Praise for the *New York Times* bestselling series

An ambitious intern.

A perfectionist executive.

And a whole lot of name calling.

"Filled with plenty of hot sex and sizzling tension . . ."

—RT Book Reviews

". . . deliciously steamy . . ."

—EW.com

"A devilishly depraved cross between a hardcore porn and a very special episode of *The Office*. . . . For us fetish-friendly fiends to feast on!!"

—PerezHilton.com

"The perfect blend of sex, sass and heart, *Beautiful Bastard* is a steamy battle of wills that will get your blood pumping!"

—S. C. Stephens, *New York Times* bestselling author of *Thoughtless*

"*Beautiful Bastard* has heart, heat, and a healthy dose of snark. Romance readers who love a smart plot are in for an amazingly sexy treat!"

—Myra McEntire, author of *Hourglass*

"*Beautiful Bastard* is the perfect mix of passionate romance and naughty eroticism. I couldn't, and didn't, put it down until I'd read every last word."

—Elena Raines, *Twilightish*

A charming British playboy.

A girl determined to finally live.

And a secret liaison revealed in all too vivid color.

"Hot . . . if you like your hook-ups early and plentiful . . ."

—EW.com

"I loved *Beautiful Bastard*, truly. I wasn't sure how Christina Lauren planned on topping Bennett . . . They did it. Max is walking hotness."

—Bookalicious

"The thing that I love the most about Christina Lauren and the duo's *Beautiful* books is that there is always humor in them. As well as hot steamy moments and some of the sweetest I love you's."

—Books She Reads

"When I say *Beautiful Stranger* is hot, I mean *Beautiful Stranger* is HOOOOOOOOOOOOTTTTTTT!!! This book has some of the steamiest, sexiest, panty-dropping scenes and dialogue of any book I've ever read."

—Live Love Laugh & Read

BOOKS BY CHRISTINA LAUREN

Beautiful Bastard

Beautiful Stranger

Beautiful Bitch

Beautiful Bombshell

Beautiful Player

Beautiful Beginning

Beautiful BOMBSHELL

CHRISTINA LAUREN

GALLERY BOOKS

NEW YORK • LONDON • TORONTO • SYDNEY • NEW DELHI

Gallery Books
A Division of Simon & Schuster, Inc.
1230 Avenue of the Americas
New York, NY 10020

This book is a work of fiction. Any references to historical events, real people, or real places are used fictitiously. Other names, characters, places, and events are products of the author's imagination, and any resemblance to actual events or places or persons, living or dead, is entirely coincidental.

First Gallery Books trade paperback edition September 2013

GALLERY BOOKS and colophon are registered trademarks of Simon & Schuster, Inc.

For information about special discounts for bulk purchases, please contact Simon & Schuster Special Sales at 1-866-506-1949 or business@simonandschuster.com.

The Simon & Schuster Speakers Bureau can bring authors to your live event. For more information or to book an event contact the Simon & Schuster Speakers Bureau at 1-866-248-3049 or visit our website at www.simonspeakers.com.

Manufactured in the United States of America

10 9 8 7 6 5

Library of Congress Cataloging-in-Publication Data
Lauren, Christina.
Beautiful Bombshell / Christina Lauren. — First Gallery Books trade paperback edition.
pages cm
1. Erotic fiction. I. Title.
PS3612.A9442273B46 2013
813'.6—dc23

2013022872

ISBN 978-1-4767-5509-0
ISBN 978-1-4767-5173-3 (ebook)

For Martha, our very own beautiful

(cancer-beating) bombshell

Beautiful BOMBSHELL

ONE

Bennett Ryan

"The smartest thing I've ever done was recruiting Max Stella to help plan your bachelor party."

I looked over at my brother, Henry, after he practically *sang* this. He was leaning back in his plush leather chair, fresh vodka gimlet in hand, recently returned from a private "session" in a mysterious backroom location, and wearing the biggest grin I think I'd ever seen. He wasn't looking at me when he spoke; he was watching three beautiful women onstage dance and strip to a slow, pulsing rhythm. "Gotta remember that next time," he murmured, bringing the glass to his lips.

"I plan on only having the one," I said.

"Well." Will Sumner, Max's best friend and business partner, leaned forward to catch Henry's eye. "*You,* however, might end up in need of a second bachelor party if the current wife finds out about the professional dancer activities just now. From the looks of this place, they don't just do the average lap wiggle around here."

With a dismissive wave of his hand, Henry said, "It really was only a lap dance." And then he smiled at me, winking. "Albeit a *very* good lap dance."

"Happy ending?" I asked, teasing but mildly revolted.

Henry shook his head with a laugh and took another sip of his drink. "Not *that* good, Ben."

I exhaled, relieved. I knew my brother well enough to know that he would never cheat on his wife, Mina, but he was still far more of the "what she doesn't know can't hurt her" ethos than I ever would be.

Although Chloe and I were getting married in June, the only weekend Max, Henry, Will, and I could all get away together for my bachelor party was the second weekend in February. We'd expected there to be some serious bribing for the women to agree to let us head to Vegas for a guy's weekend over Valentine's Day, but as usual they'd surprised us: they'd barely blinked, and simply planned a weekend trip to the Catskills together instead.

Max had chosen a high-end club to kick off the weekend of ensured debauchery. This place certainly wasn't something we would have stumbled upon via an online search or a stroll down the Las Vegas Strip. To be honest, Black Heart didn't look like much from the outside. It was buried in an innocuous office building a couple blocks off the heavy traffic of Las Vegas Boulevard. But inside—past three locked doors and two bouncers roughly the size of my apartment in New York, then deeper into the dark belly of the building—the club was posh, and positively vibrating with sex.

The enormous main room was spotted with small raised platforms, each one topped with a dancer wearing sparkling, silver lingerie. There were four black marble bars, one in every corner, and each specializing in a different type of drink. Henry and I had indulged in the vodka bar, also grabbing some caviar, gravlax, and blinis. Max and Will had made a beeline for the scotch. The other two bars offered an assortment of wine, or cordials.

The furniture was plush, dark leather. It was unbelievably soft, and each chair was large enough for two . . . in case any of us accepted the offers for a dance out on the main floor. Servers wearing anything from latex bikinis to nothing at all carried trays with drinks. Our hostess, Gia, had started the night in a lacy red chemise and panties with some elaborate jewelry in her hair, ears, and around her neck, but seemed to be removing something each time she checked on us.

I wasn't a regular at this type of establishment, but even I knew this was no run-of-the-mill strip club. It was pretty fucking impressive.

"The question," Henry said, interrupting my thoughts, "is when is the groom-to-be getting his lap dance?"

Around me, the others all responded with various words of encouragement, but I was already shaking my head. "I'm going to pass. Lap dances aren't really my thing."

"How is an unfamiliar and extremely hot woman dancing on your lap not your thing?" Henry asked, eyes wide with disbelief. My brother and I hadn't ever visited a club of this sort in any of our business travels. I think I was as surprised to learn of his enthusiasm for them as he was to learn of my aversion. "Are you warm-blooded?"

I nodded. "Very. I think that's why I don't like them."

"Bollocks," Max said, putting his drink down on the table and waving across the room to someone in the far, dark corner. "This is the first night of your stag weekend, and a lappy is a requisite."

"You may all be surprised to hear that I'm with Bennett on this one," Will said. "Lap dances from strangers are pretty awful. Where do you put your hands? Where do you look? It's not the same as being with a lover—it feels too impersonal."

While Henry insisted that Will had obviously never had a good lap dance, Max stood to speak to a man who seemed to have materialized out of thin air at the side of our table. He was shorter than Max—which wasn't uncommon—and graying at his temples. He had a face and eyes that carried the kind of calm that told me he'd done a lot, and seen even more. His suit was dark and impeccable, his lips pressed together in a thin line. I registered that this must be the infamous Johnny French, whom Max had mentioned on our flight in.

Although I'd assumed they were talking about making arrangements for me to get a dance, I watched as Johnny murmured something and Max turned to stare at the wall, his face tight. I could count on one hand the number of times I'd ever seen Max look anything but relaxed, and I leaned forward, straining to understand what was happening. Henry and Will remained oblivious, having returned their attention to the now-naked dancers on the stage. Finally, Max's shoulders relaxed as if he had come to some kind of conclusion, and he smiled at Johnny, muttering, "Thanks, mate."

With a pat to Max's shoulder, Johnny turned and left us. Max returned to his seat, reaching for his drink. I lifted my chin toward the doorway Johnny had stepped through, behind a black curtain. "What was all that about?"

"That," said Max, "was about the room that is being prepared for you."

"For *me*?" I pressed my hand to my chest, shaking my head. "Again, Max, I'm going to pass."

"The fuck you are."

"You're serious."

"You're bloody right I am. He told me you're to head down that hall"—Max pointed to a different doorway than the one through which Johnny had disappeared—"and head to Neptune."

I groaned, leaning back in my chair. Although this club seemed like the best of its kind in town—or anywhere for that matter—on a list of things I wanted to do tonight, getting a lap dance from some random Vegas dancer ranked barely above eating bad sushi and getting violently ill.

"Just walk down the hall like a fucking bloke and get your knob rubbed by some girl dancing on you." Max stared at me, his eyes narrowed. "Are you taking the piss with this whingey shite? It's your fucking *stag weekend.* Act like the man you used to be."

I studied him, wondering why he seemed so firmly planted in his own chair while he encouraged me to leave mine. "Did Johnny give you a room to visit as well? Aren't you getting a lap dance?"

He laughed, tipping his scotch to his lips and mumbling, "It's a lap dance, Ben. Not a fucking trip to the dentist."

"Asshole." Lifting my drink, I gazed at the thick, clear liquid. I'd known going into this that there would be women, and booze, and probably some activities that might push the limits of legal, but the truth was, Chloe had known this, too. She'd told me to have fun, and her eyes had never shadowed with worry or mistrust. They had no reason to.

I brought the drink to my lips, downed it, and muttered, "Fuck it," before standing and heading to the hallway. My companions for the evening were—surprisingly—classy enough to not cheer at my departure, but even still I could feel their attention on my back as I made my way to the hallway to the left of the main stage.

Just beyond the doorway the carpet changed from black

to a deep, royal blue, and the space felt even darker than it had out in the main room. The walls were the same velvety black, and there was just enough illumination from tiny crystal lights on the wall to light a path ahead of me. Along one side of the long hallway were doors with the names of planets on them: Mercury, Venus, Earth . . . Down at the end, at the door labeled Neptune, I hesitated. Would there be a woman already inside? Would there be a chair for me or, worse, a *bed*?

The door was ornate and heavy, like something out of a castle or, fuck, some sort of creepy Gothic basement sex dungeon. *Fucking Max.* I shivered and turned the knob, exhaling in relief when I saw that there was no iron cross or handcuffs, and no woman inside yet, only a long chaise with a small silver box in its center. Tied to the box with a silky red ribbon was a white card with *Bennett Ryan* written in neat script.

Great. Random Vegas Dancer might already know my fucking name.

Inside the box was a black satin blindfold and a sliver of thick cardstock with the words *Put this on* written in black ink.

I was meant to put on a blindfold for a *lap* dance? What was the point of that? Just because I didn't want one tonight didn't mean I didn't recall lap dances past. Unless the format had changed in the past few years, getting one meant looking, not touching. What the fuck was I supposed to do if I was blindfolded when she came in? I sure as shit wasn't going to touch her.

I laid the slip of fabric on the chaise, ignoring it as I stared at the wall. Minutes ticked by, and with each one I grew more convinced there was no fucking way I was blindfolding myself in this room.

I could almost hear the sound of my own irritation building. It sounded like a roar, a wave, a flame crackling. Closing my eyes, I took three deep breaths and then looked more carefully at my surroundings. The walls were a soft gray, the chaise a dusky blue. The room looked more like a dressing room at a high-end store than a room where men got what I assumed amounted to a lot more than *just a dance*. I ran my hand over the supple leather of the chaise, and only then did I notice the second note that had been buried beneath the blindfold inside the box. Written in the same script on the heavy paper, it said,

Put on the fucking blindfold, Ben, don't be a pussy.

Fucking *Max*. Would I really have to sit here, captive, until I put on the blindfold and got this over with? With a groan, I lifted the black fabric, slipping it over my head and hesitating just a heartbeat before pulling it across my eyes. I was already plotting how I would get back at Max. He'd known me longer than almost anyone in my life other than my family, and was aware of how much I valued fidelity and control. Asking me to come back to this room and cover my eyes without knowing what was coming? What a fucking *dick*.

I leaned back against the wall and waited in annoyed isolation, my ears picking up sounds I hadn't noticed before: the dull pulse of the music in the other rooms, the sound of doors opening and closing with quiet, heavy clicks. And then I heard the sound of the handle to my room turning, the door opening with the gentle slide of wood across carpeting.

My heart began to thunder.

As soon as I got a whiff of the unfamiliar perfume, I felt my back go rigid with discomfort. Other than the scent of the stranger, I knew nothing about who was in here and I hated not being able to see what was coming at me. She did something against the wall: I heard rustling, a small click, and then quiet, rhythmic music filled the room.

Warm, soft hands took hold of my wrists and gently but expertly positioned my hands so that they rested idly at my sides. *No touching? No fucking problem.*

I sat motionless as she slid over me, her breath smelling like cinnamon, her hips grinding on my lap, hands pressed to my chest. So this is how it was going to go: I would remain blindfolded, she would dance over me, and then I would leave? I felt myself begin to relax incrementally. The woman moved above me, her hips shifting against my thighs, her hands moving gently over my chest. I could feel enough of her body that the blindfold didn't seem completely absurd, but if I'd been the kind of man to enjoy this sort of thing, being robbed of my sight would have been a hindrance.

But maybe Max knew this would be the only way this experience wouldn't be unbearable to me. The thought made me want to kick his ass just slightly less.

The dancer rolled over me, hips rocking rhythmically with the music, undulating in small, suggestive circles. She leaned away, gripping my shoulders to anchor herself, and I felt the press of her ass on my thighs, the suggestion of her sex so close to my dick that I tried as carefully as I could to inch away, to push my body deeper into the chaise. And then she sat upright again, and I could feel the shape of her breasts as she brushed against my chest. Her breath was warm and soft on my neck, and although it wasn't unpleasant, per se, it quickly grew awkward. My initial fear that I would have to make eye contact, or smile, or appear to be here voluntarily dissolved, and instead I registered that this dance was for *neither* of us. Certainly she wasn't getting anything but money out of it, and because of my blindfold, I didn't even need to fake my enjoyment. I found myself straining to calculate how much was left of the song. It wasn't one I knew, but the formula was clear and I exhaled the rest of my tension as the song started its predictable ramp-up to the end. Over me, the poor woman seemed to slow, her hands coming to rest on my shoulders.

When the song ended, the only sound remaining in the room was the stripper's quickened breathing.

Is she going to leave? Should I say something?

With dread weighing down my stomach, I understood very clearly that maybe *this* was when the show really started. To my absolute horror, the stripper leaned forward and grazed her teeth across my jaw.

Then . . . I froze, a cloudy awareness starting to overtake my impatience.

"Hello, Mr. Ryan." Her breath was hot in my ear and I startled at the sound, my entire body going stiff. *What in the actual fuck?* My hands curled into fists at my sides. "I really, *really* want to kiss that sexy, angry mouth of yours."

I opened my mouth to speak, but nothing came out.

Chloe Fucking Mills.

"I just danced my ass off, and you aren't even a little hard right now?" She leaned in, licking up my neck as she lowered her hips and wiggled over my cock. "There we go . . ." She giggled into my neck. "*Now* you are."

My mind exploded with reactions: relief and anger, shock and embarrassment. Here Chloe was, in Vegas, not skiing in the fucking Catskills, and she'd come in here to find me blindfolded and waiting for a dancer to do exactly what she'd done: dance on my thighs, grind herself into my cock. But for once I'd managed to do with Chloe what I'd been able to do in every one of my business relationships*: hide the reaction you have until you've transformed it into the reaction you want.*

I counted down from ten before asking, "Was this some sort of test?"

She leaned close, kissed my earlobe. "No."

I wasn't going to explain why I was in this room; I'd done nothing wrong. Still, I felt the strange war inside me: growing arousal that she'd done this for me and anger that she'd set me up. "You're in trouble, Mills."

She pressed a fingertip to my lips, and then trapped it between our mouths with a brief kiss. "I'm just happy to be right. Max owes me fifty dollars. I told him you would hate getting a lap dance from a stranger. Your hard limit is infidelity."

I swallowed, nodding.

"I used all of my moves, but *nothing*. Not even a twitch down there. I'm really hoping you had no idea it was me or else—I'll be honest—I'm a little insulted."

Shaking my head, I murmured, "No. The perfume is . . . off. You hate cinnamon gum. And I can't see you or feel you."

"You can now," she said, lifting my hands to rest on her bare thighs. I ran my palms up to her hips and felt the sharp press of small stones on her underwear. *What the fuck is she wearing?* I was dying to take off the blindfold, but as she hadn't done it yet, I suspected this was another thing I was meant to wait for.

I ran my hands over her thighs, down to her calves, and suddenly wanted nothing more than to get laid in this room in the middle of a questionably legal Vegas club. My relief that it was Chloe in here with me, and not some stranger sitting on my lap, overwhelmed me, and a burst of adrenaline shot into my bloodstream. "You should feel free to fuck me in this room, Miss Mills."

She leaned forward, sucked on my jaw. "Hmm . . . maybe. Want a second chance to enjoy a dance first?"

I nodded and exhaled as she slipped the blindfold off me, exposing her . . . *outfit*. She wore a tiny bra that tied with thin satin straps at her shoulders and appeared to be made entirely of gemstones held together with the barest scrap of silk. Her panties were similarly flimsy, and even more fascinating. The thin satin ties at the sides hinted to me that I probably shouldn't destroy them.

Running a fingertip across her torso, she whispered, "You like my new lingerie?"

I stared at the tiny jewels decorating her skin, winking brilliant green and clear as diamonds. She looked like a fucking work of art. "They'll do," I mumbled, leaning forward to kiss between her breasts. "In a pinch."

"Do you want to touch me?"

I nodded again, looking up at her face and feeling my eyes grow dark at the way she watched me with both hunger and uncertainty.

She smiled, licked her lips. "This wasn't a test, sending you down here. But," she said, eyes falling to my mouth, "the fact is that you *did* come down to this room expecting a stranger to dance for you. You put on a blindfold, and any other woman could have come in here and touched what's mine." She cocked her head, studied me. "I think maybe I deserve a little treat."

Hell yes. "I can agree with that."

"And, the rules being what they are"—she nodded to a small sign on the wall basically suggesting that men who violated dancers would be unceremoniously carried out and dropped over the Hoover Dam—"you still aren't allowed to touch me freely."

I wasn't sure what she meant by "freely" and I was still mostly trapped beneath her, so I simply let my hands fall back to her thighs, waiting for instruction. My body was tightly coiled and ready for whatever she wanted to do.

She stood, walked over to the wall unit, and started the song over again.

I really was a lucky fucking bastard. I had the hottest girlfriend in the entire world. Licking my lips, I stared at her firm, perfect ass until she turned back around and, with the trademark confident sway of her hips, returned to where I sat.

Chloe climbed over me, straddling my thighs. "Take off my panties."

I pulled at the delicate tie at each hip, and slowly dragged them away from her body, tossing them to the side somewhere.

"Now. Put the back of your hand on your thigh and hold up however many fingers you want me to fuck," she whispered.

I blinked. *"What?"*

She laughed, sucking on her lip before enunciating very slowly, "Put the back of your *hand* on your *thigh,* and hold up however many *fingers* you want me to *fuck."*

Was she serious with this shit? Without taking my eyes off of hers, I slid my hand to my leg, turned it palm up, and offered up my middle finger. "Here you go."

She looked down and giggled. "That's a good one, but maybe at least one more. I *do* need a closer approximation of your cock."

"You're really only going to fuck my *fingers*? My dick is pretty much ready to go, and you can't pretend that isn't the preferable option for everyone involved."

"You were going to get a lap dance from a Vegas showgirl," she countered, brow raised. "Your dick wasn't even interested five minutes ago."

With a sigh, I closed my eyes, extending three fingers.

"So generous," she whispered, lifting her hips and gliding her sex across my rigid fingertips. "You'll make a pretty stellar husband if you keep this sort of thing up."

"Chlo . . ." I groaned, opening my eyes to watch her as she slowly lowered herself over my fingers. She was already wet, and I stared down at her, naked but for her skimpy bra, her smooth thighs spread over the dark fabric of my pants.

She wrapped her hands around my neck and began to move over me, lifting her body and circling her hips as she came down, rubbing her clit against the heel of my hand.

Again, and again, and again. I thrust up beneath her, needing friction. I could taste her scent in the air, could hear every one of her tight little sounds. Between her breasts, sweat caused her skin to glisten. No way would I admit right now how much I loved watching her use my body to find her own pleasure.

"You're a fucking tease," I growled, relishing the dip and swell from the weight of her arms braced on my shoulders. The sight of her was doing savage things to my body, and I was pretty sure I could get off if she just lowered herself a bit more, rubbed her thigh against my clothed cock. "I'm going to walk out of here still hard and smelling like pussy."

Circling her hips, she whispered, "Don't care."

And yet, at the sound of my voice, I'd noticed the tight press of her nipples inside her little bra. She knew how hard I was, and she cared *greatly.*

Chloe gasped as I curled my fingers and moved my other hand to slide over her backside and guide her hips. I pressed my thumb across her clit, feeling myself come undone just watching her. Around my fingers, her body rippled, tensing in anticipation. Even in a strange room with God-knows-what going on around us, I could make her come in minutes. She was such a fucking tangle of contradictions: generous and teasing, earnest and coy. "You fucking *wreck* me, Chlo."

"Can you tell I'm close?" Our eyes never broke contact, and I slid my hand up her side, tracing the frame of her ribs with my fingertips.

"Yeah," I whispered.

"Does that still make you wild? Knowing how fast you can do this to me?"

I nodded, and my hand slid higher, to her shoulder, her neck. My fingers flexed against her jugular, itching to feel the race of her pulse when she came. "I love knowing no one else could make you this wet."

Her brown sugar eyes darkened, grew heavy with desire. "I need you to want me every second," she whispered, breathless. "You're the only one I'd ever let own me like this."

The word—*own*—triggered a spark in my chest, a wildness I couldn't hold back anymore. Her lips were so close to mine and the taste of cinnamon on her breath, the foreign perfume . . . the reality of how far she'd gone to fool me poured fuel on the flame and I lurched forward, disintegrating; my kiss was sharp and punishing, starving for the feel and taste of her.

She pulled back only far enough to gasp, "Do you want to hear me?"

"I want the entire club to hear you."

Her hands sank into the hair at the nape of my neck and her hips faltered, trapping my fingers deep inside her as she rocked wildly over my palm.

"Oh *God* . . . " Pulling her bottom lip into her mouth, she arched away and I bent to her neck, sucking, biting, *owning* her fucking heartbeat.

I felt the hammering of her pulse against my lips, felt each one of her exhales as she gasped, tensing above me and around me as she came. With a hoarse cry, she said my name and her voice sent a vibration across my tongue, pressed to her throat.

Chloe stilled, her body leaning into mine, sated and boneless, and lifted both hands to my neck. Her thumbs pressed gently into my pulse points and she leaned forward, sucking my lower lip into her mouth before biting it quickly, savagely. I let out a surprised grunt, and wasn't sure what it said about me that for a second I thought that bite might make me come in my pants.

"That . . . " she breathed, pulling back, "was *unbelievable*."

Lifting herself gingerly off my hand, she rose and stood on shaky legs. I leaned forward to kiss the damp skin between her breasts, and pulled her hand over the crown of my cock through my pants. "You're so fucking beautiful when you come, Chlo. Feel how hard you get me."

She squeezed, stroking me slowly.

My eyes rolled closed and I begged, "I want you on your knees now. Put your mouth on me."

But to my absolute fucking horror, she moved her hand and walked over to retrieve her panties from the corner.

"What are you doing?" I rasped.

She tied the tiny straps of satin at each hip, and pulled a

robe from a hook on the wall, slipping it over her shoulders and smiling a little at me. "You good?"

I returned her level stare. "Are you *serious*?"

She came back to me, lifting my left hand to her mouth, sliding my bare ring finger between her teeth and deeper, wrapping it in the delicate softness of her tongue. And then she released it with a wink, whispering, "I'm serious."

My arms shook with tension, my cock pulsing from the echo of her mouth, her too-short, gentle suction. "Then no, I am *not* good, Chloe. Not even a little bit."

"I am," she said, smiling sweetly. "I feel *fantastic*. I hope you enjoy the rest of your bachelor party."

I leaned back into the wall, watching her cinch the robe around her waist. My skin felt hot, itchy, feverish and the entire time she dressed she watched me, relishing my frustrated need for her.

I struggled to hide it, deciding to pretend I was fine. Yelling would only make her more pleased with herself. Cool detachment always worked best when Chloe was being a teasing bitch. But when my brow smoothed, she laughed a little, not even a little surprised.

"What are you doing after this?" I asked. For some reason it hadn't even occurred to me what she would do when she left. Was she flying straight home?

With a shrug, she murmured, "Don't know. Dinner. Maybe a show."

"Wait. Are you here with someone?"

She looked at me, pursing her lips and shrugging.

"The fuck, Chloe? Are you at least going to tell me where you're *staying*?"

She looked me up and down, letting her eyes linger a little longer on the fly of my pants than the rest of me before she smiled. "At a *hotel*." She straightened, arching her brow before purring, "Oh, and happy Valentine's Day, Mr. Ryan."

And with that, she stepped out of the room and into the hallway.

Two

Max Stella

Bennett Ryan looked like he was on the verge of losing his lunch and razzing all over the table.

"I'm going to pass. Lap dances aren't really my thing."

His brother Henry leaned forward, horrified. "How is an unfamiliar and extremely hot woman dancing on your lap not your thing? Are you warm-blooded?"

Bennett mumbled some excuse, and I couldn't really blame him because, fuck, I wasn't about to have some strange bird climb on my cock. But he had no idea what was waiting on him in the back. I had to get him out of that bloody chair and into the private room so we could get this night started off right.

"Bollocks," I told him, waving to where Johnny stood, waiting near the private hallway. "This is your bachelor party, and a lappy is a requisite."

Johnny raised his chin in acknowledgment and finished his conversation with security before making his way through the room, taking his sweet bloody time. Every second that ticked by saw my own impatience build. The longer it took Johnny to get here, the longer it would take Ben to man up and head back, and the longer my girl waited for me.

When he finally stood in front of me, Johnny flashed me a knowing smile. "Heya, Max. How can I help you?"

"I think we're ready to begin the festivities."

Johnny nodded, slipping a hand into his pocket. "Chloe is in Neptune. Down the Blue Hallway, to the left of the stage."

I nodded, waiting. Finally, when he hadn't offered more information, I prompted, "And Sara?"

"She's in the Green Room, down the Black Hallway. The one to the *right* of the stage," Johnny said. He leaned in a little to add, "Positioned how she requested."

I stopped short, slipping my hand into my pocket to hide the fist that had instinctively formed. "She asked you to *position* her?" What in the bloody hell did that even *mean*?

"Just a little ribbon here, a little ribbon there." Johnny watched me, a small grin giving away how amused he was by my reaction.

I looked around the dark room, at the scattered clients sitting on black leather couches or leaning against the sleek charcoal granite bar. I could feel my pulse in my jaw from clenching my teeth together in what I knew was an uncharacteristic scowl.

I was conflicted: curious at this growth in their trust, but needing to know what he'd seen, and *where* he'd touched her. It was rare for Sara to be tied up at Red Moon, and each time, it had been *my* doing. "She let you touch her?"

Johnny looked at me, smiling wider as he rocked on his heels. "Yep."

He didn't shrink under my heated attention. He just let me ride over the hot flash of jealousy, knowing that more than anything I was filled with gratitude. Over the past nine months or so, Johnny had done so much for us, and even through my haze of anger, I knew it wasn't a simple favor he was doing for me tonight, with both Chloe and Sara taking up valuable rooms in his busy club.

I looked over at him, smiled. "Right then. Thanks, mate."

Johnny patted my shoulder, nodded at someone behind me, and murmured, "Have fun tonight, Max. You have an hour before the next show goes into the Green Room." With that, he turned and returned to the Black Hallway, the one where I would also find Sara, in *position,* with *ribbon.*

I felt the frenetic longing grow in my chest. A tightening; the way I feel at the start of a rugby match . . . but deeper inside me, and *everywhere.* It spread from my thorax out to the end of every limb, pulsing hotly in each fingertip. I needed to get to her, give her what she'd begged to come to Vegas to do.

When I told Sara that the only weekend we could do Bennett's bachelor party was Valentine's weekend, her first reaction was to laugh and remind me that she hated Valentine's Day. Her ex had always fucked it up, she'd said, and I was secretly pleased she didn't want to make a thing of it anyway. We celebrated our relationship almost every fucking night in my bed, and most *definitely* every Wednesday night in our room at Red Moon. Valentine's Day was an insignificant blurb on the calendar compared to all that.

But Sara's second, lingering reaction was to step closer, run her hands up my chest, and ask if she could come, too. "I promise I won't crash the rest of the party," she whispered, eyes wide and mysteriously combining uncertainty and lust. "The bachelor weekend can go on as planned; I just want to play at Black Heart one time."

Before I could even find the single word to answer her, I'd bent to kiss her, and that kiss had transformed into her hands in my hair and my mouth on her tits. And that had moved on to hard and fast sex on my kitchen counter. Afterward, I'd collapsed onto her, panting against the damp skin of her neck: "Fuck yes, you can come to Vegas."

Rearranging my features into something calmer, I sat back down and felt Bennett's attention on my face as I picked up my drink.

"What was all that about?" he asked, watching Johnny disappear behind the black rope.

"That," I answered, "was about the room that is being prepared for you."

"For me?" Bennett pressed a hand to his chest, already resisting. "Again, Max, I'm going to pass."

I groaned, giving him a skeptical glance. "The fuck you are."

"You're serious."

We argued a bit longer, until I could see him give in. His face grew determined and he hesitated, contemplating his vodka, and then downed it.

"Fuck it." He put his glass down, shot up from his chair, and marched determined down the hall.

It was all I could do to not similarly bolt from my seat. Sara's name echoed in my every heartbeat. I loved her so wildly, it was a wonder this wasn't also my stag weekend. The number of times I'd almost proposed to her was bordering on absurd. And somehow, I knew she could see it in my face: that moment when I started to beg her to leave for the weekend with me, marry me, move in with me . . . and then thought better of it. Without fail, she asked what I had meant to say, and I told her she looked beautiful instead of releasing the words, *"I'm not going to feel sorted until we're married."*

I often had to remind myself it had been a mere six months—almost nine including our initial arrangement—and Sara was skittish about all things matrimonial. She'd kept her apartment, but honestly I don't know why she bothered. For the first month or two after we reconciled, we'd split our time at the two places, but my home was larger, better furnished, and my bedroom had better lighting for the photographs I loved to take of her. Soon she was in my bed every night of the week. She would be mine forever, but—fuck—I had to remind myself we didn't need to rush it.

After what felt like an appropriate amount of time since Bennett left, I put my own tumbler on the table and looked up at Will and Henry.

"Gentlemen," I began, "I'm headed down the hall to have a fabulous Vegas bird dance on my lap."

Both barely looked away from the dancers on the stage, and I was fairly confident I could leave and they wouldn't think to look which hall I was headed down.

The hall to the left of the stage led to private rooms named after the planets. These rooms were for lap dances mainly, much like the one Bennett was currently getting. In my opinion, the only interesting thing in those rooms tonight was the fact that he was getting his dance from Chloe.

But the rooms to the right of the stage, labeled simply by color, were for an altogether different purpose. No one could enter those save for certain club employees and a very select group of clientele. The roped-off section was for the patrons who paid for the privilege of watching sex acts. Much like Red Moon in New York, Black Heart in Vegas catered in part to a population of the rich and passionately voyeuristic.

As I'd expected, neither of my mates looked up as I stood, moved around the back of our group of plush leather chairs, and slid first to the back of the room before moving to the far side wall. Even if they weren't looking, I still didn't need to provoke their attention by making a beeline for the private hallway.

I moved along the wall to the front, where a man almost my height stood, wearing a black suit and an earpiece. With a nod, he unlatched the heavy silk rope and let me pass through the thick velvet curtain.

I had full access. None of my partners in crime were to be allowed back here, however, no matter how influential or smooth-talking the Ryan brothers were. I'd made Johnny promise they would not accidentally stumble upon me and Sara.

I'd been in Red Moon so many times with her now

that I didn't need to see inside any of the other rooms to know what I'd find there.

In the Red Room, a naked woman being whipped by one man while another dripped hot candle wax over her breasts.

In the White Room, a man's hand up to the wrist disappearing inside a woman lying spread eagle on a table.

In the Pink Room, I caught a glimpse of three women, all making love to the same man.

The carpet was thick, silencing my steps. Here, unlike at Red Moon, the one-way windows looking in on each room were smaller, though there were more of them. It gave the feeling of seeing a different show through each one, a different view of the same scene: standard voyeuristic fare. I'd learned in the past few months that the performers—while fetish-driven and daring—rarely portrayed anything beyond graphic, emotionless fucking. Which was fine; according to Johnny, most patrons wanted only to see the extreme sex acts, things they wouldn't find on television or—indeed—their own bedroom.

But there were the few, our unknown regulars at Red Moon, who came on Wednesdays specifically to watch me with Sara. Our nights there came above almost any other obligation, whether it was work or friends or family; Red Moon let us express something we both needed. In the past months, we had fully embraced our shared exhibitionist fetish, discussing it for hours afterward in her bed or mine.

There wasn't anyone watching our room yet when I approached, so I could slip in unnoticed. As I knew it would be, the door to the Green Room was unlocked. No patron allowed back here other than me would dare try a stray doorknob in one of Johnny's clubs.

It was a small room, like all the others, empty but for two props: a plain metal chair and table. The empty décor meant that every ounce of my attention—and the attention of anyone watching from the hallway—would be drawn to the naked woman currently bent over the table.

She was blindfolded. The curve of her perfect ass lifted in the air. Her spine was straight and relaxed. When the door clicked shut behind me, she pulled her lower lip into her mouth, and I could see a shudder pass through her body.

"It's me, Petal."

She didn't need me to say it. I could tell from her posture that she'd known who had come in, but I wanted to reassure her anyway. She looked completely relaxed, her head turned to the side, cheek resting on the table, and I took a moment to let my eyes move over her.

Each ankle was tied to a table leg with the ribbon

Johnny had mentioned, spreading her wide enough for me to have my way with her however I liked. She was bent at the waist, her hands tied loosely behind her back. Her skin was smooth and flawless, her mouth wet and slightly open now. I scanned her body again and, as if she could sense where I directed my attention, she pushed her ass a little higher.

I moved to her, pressing my palm to the skin between her shoulder blades. She jumped a little, moaning in pleasure, as my hand slid down her spine and over the curve of her backside.

"You look fucking *beautiful,* darling."

"Your hand is cold," she whispered. "It feels so good."

Indeed, her skin was hot. I imagined she was flushed from excitement and the anticipation of not knowing when I would show up, and not knowing who might see her before I did. I slid a finger down her ass and lower, dipping into the source of her wetness. She was already slick. My cock grew rigid at the sight of her, the feel of her seduction on my fingers. When I slid two deep inside her, she jerked on the table, and I was relieved to notice Johnny hadn't tied her up very tightly.

Sara had finally met Johnny by daylight soon after she'd come back to me, last August. Although they had been introduced briefly after our first scene at his club, Sara wanted to sit down with him away from that whole world; she said it would make her feel more comfortable about what we were doing if she could see the man behind it all. We joined him for coffee in a tiny coffee shop in Brooklyn. Johnny—like the rest of us—had been smitten the moment Sara had leaned into him and kissed his cheek, openly thanking him for everything he did for us.

They just *clicked.* He understood her from the moment he saw her, in a way I think only I had before. He was crazy for her, protective of her, and—as of this evening—was the only man other than me she would ever let touch her, and even then only to prepare her for this special occasion. The trust she gave him was a testament to her faith in me as well.

I took in her cream curves, the starkness of the red ribbon around her wrists and ankles, the strong, smooth line of her spine. My chest constricted with an ache so deep, when I tried to speak my voice came out a touch strangled. "How long have you been here?"

She gave a little shrug. "Johnny left maybe ten minutes ago. He said you would be here soon."

I nodded, bending to kiss her shoulder. "And here I am."

"Here you are."

"Was it hard to wait?"

She licked her lips before answering, "No."

"A few people are down at the next room," I told

her, kissing down her back. "I imagine they walked past this room and saw you alone in here, waiting."

She shivered against me, exhaling a tight burst of air.

"I bet you knew that. I bet you bloody *loved* it."

She nodded.

"You know how much I love you?"

Again, she nodded, and a blush spread from her neck down her back. More than anything, Sara craved the knowledge that someone was watching us make love. She wasn't very often tied up for me; sometimes she was in charge, climbing on top and sliding down over me, or taking me in her mouth. In those times she liked to watch my face. Her eyes would take in every one of my fascinated reactions, as if it was still hard for her to believe how obliterated I was by her affection.

But sometimes—only a handful of nights at Johnny's club—she wanted to be blindfolded, left to imagine how I looked when I saw her, and felt her, and fucked her.

I reached up, untying the ribbon around her wrists, and felt a bit like I was unwrapping a gift. Sara flexed her hands and then slid her arms up, reaching to curl her fingers around the far edge of the table.

"Did you know I was going to suggest you do that?"

She smiled over her shoulder at my general direction, the blindfold keeping me from her sight. "I had an inkling."

And then we both heard it at the same time: a crash in the hall, the sound of someone dropping what must have been an entire tray of drinks. We'd never been certain when we were being watched before. At Red Moon, the rooms were soundproofed; here, the walls were thick but not as insulated.

In front of me, Sara shivered, her back arching.

"Apparently they plan to stay long enough to have some drinks delivered." I took off my suit jacket, folding it over the back of the chair before I bent and slid my hands between the table and her body, palms up to cup her breasts. "Beautiful girl." I kissed her shoulder, her neck, and down her back, letting my hands slide down the front of her. Licking, nibbling; I couldn't get enough of her fucking beautiful skin.

"Bloody brilliant," I whispered, pulling the metal chair close enough for me to sit down and press my teeth into the curve of her ass. "Think we only have time for a tiny taste." With my hands on the back of her thighs, I spread her open, bending forward to kiss her clit, taste where she was warm and sweet.

"Max." Her voice was strained, wrapped tight around the single syllable.

"Hmm?" I tasted her again, letting my eyes fall closed. "You're so perfect right here." I kissed her right where she would take me inside. "Right fucking *here*."

"Please. Now." Her thighs trembled in my hands.

"You don't want to come on my mouth?" I asked, already pushing to stand and unfastening my belt.

"I know we don't have a lot of time. I want to feel you inside before you have to leave."

Pushing my boxers down my thighs, I teased at her entrance, sliding my cock up and over her clit. "Before we begin, I need your thoughts on something."

She moaned, pushing back into me. "Need to know where to put it?"

I bent and kissed her back, laughing. "No, you naughty fucking girl. This will be too quick for that."

She licked her lips, waiting.

Poised just barely inside her, I asked, "Shall I take you bare? I do have a condom in my pocket."

Her breath hitched. "Bare."

My chest squeezed and I stared down at her, wanting to absorb the moment just a little fucking longer. She was tied to a table, naked and ready for me. My silk tie dragged along her spine as I bent over her, and the deep blue contrasted perfectly with the pale flush of her skin. Bloody hell, she was hot. We never used condoms at home, but here in the club and with her whole night ahead of her, it was a little different.

I slid in so slowly I felt every fucking centimeter of her stretching for me. She cried out, tilting her hips up to take me deeply. In this position, with the difference in our heights, I could curl along the entire length of her spine and speak right into her ear. "Are you sure?"

"I'm sure."

"Because now I've just pushed inside you, with no protection, Petal. If I *come* inside you, the drink-spillers out there will know you belong to me."

She moaned, fingers curling right around the edge of the table. "And?"

"And you'll have my come inside you after I leave; is that what you like?"

"You'll know it's there," she whispered, rocking up to meet my movements. "*That's* what I'll like. When you're out there, sitting with the boys, or at dinner later, you'll be thinking about how I can still feel you."

"Too fucking right." I slid my hand around her hips and pressed my fingers all along her sex, giving her friction everywhere.

I started slow, teasing, watching myself disappear and emerge, wet with her. But the reality of the night pressed in on my little private bubble and I knew I didn't have hours to relish this. This would be quick pleasure only; I would find time to drink her in much more slowly later.

She gasped when I pulled back and returned to her roughly, building a rhythm so hard and fast the table squeaked on the floor, the hinges groaned. Sara took it all with her perfect arse in the air, pushing back into me as hard and fast as I moved forward.

With a quiet moan, she whispered, "Max, I'm there."

I circled my fingers over her clit, pressed harder, moved faster. I knew this woman's body as well as my own. Knew how fast she needed it, how hard. Knew how much she loved the sound of her name in my voice.

"Petal," I groaned. "I'm dying to feel you come around my cock."

Arching her neck, she pressed the back of her head into my shoulder, letting out a smooth, effortless moan. "More. More."

"I fucking love you, Sara."

That did it; her fingers gripped the table edge so hard her knuckles went white, and her orgasm surged around me, pulled from her in the same rhythm as her hot little sounds.

"What are you feeling?" I managed, lips pressed just below her ear. "Power? Control? Here you are, blindfolded and tied to a table and I'm fucking *lost* in you. I'm so fucking lost I can barely catch my breath."

Exhaling heavily, she seemed to sink into the table, sated. "Love."

My release teased along my back, hovered low in my stomach as my hips sped up. "'Love'?" I repeated. "You're tied to a metal table, having just orgasmed in front of God knows who, and you feel love. . . . You must be lost in me just the same."

She turned her head, capturing my lips. Sara gave me her mouth, her tongue, her hoarse hungry sounds, and I was done for, groaning as I lost my rhythm, my hips slapping her backside as I grew fevered until finally, my whole body tensed in release.

I stilled, dizzy and relishing the feel of her kisses when she was like this, slow and languid after her orgasm. The room disappeared, and as clichéd as it sounded, time stopped. Everything in this night became about her body, and her lips, her eyes opening and meeting mine as we kissed.

Slowly, I pulled from her, and forced her lips to slow their soft, hungry assault so I could just enjoy the shape of her mouth. I ran two fingers over her pussy, relishing the way she jerked beneath me. Pressing two fingers inside her, I could still feel the heat of the friction, the evidence of my pleasure.

"Dirty fucking girl," I whispered, pushing deep into her.

I tugged my fingers back and smiled at the way her body seemed unwilling to let me go.

But she needed to stand, and stretch; and I needed to carry on with my night.

I stood, fixing my trousers, and then kneeled to untie her legs. She straightened, arching her back before turning and pushing up to sit on the table, pulling me by my tie to stand between her legs.

"What are you guys doing next?" she asked, smoothing her hands over my dress shirt.

"Dinner, I believe." I stepped away only long enough to retrieve her robe from the corner of the room. I was done letting others look at her. "And you?"

"Dinner," she said, shrugging. "Then I'm not sure." She looked up, gave me a teasing little smile. "Maybe we'll go to another club."

"And what?" I asked, laughing. "Watch some blokes in banana hammocks wiggle their tackle in your face? No, Petal."

Her eyes widened in slight challenge. "Well, you go have your fun night, I'll go have mine."

With a smile, I leaned in to kiss her, letting her deepen it with her hands on my face, sliding into my hair and around the back of my neck. "I feel like I could fuck for hours," she whispered into my mouth, and I almost lost it right then; Sara rarely swore, and when she did, it always made me hard. "I just feel a little hollow with how much I want you tonight."

I groaned and pressed my face into her neck.

"I know, I know," she murmured, and when she pressed her hands to my chest, I stepped back so she could stand. "I'm sure Chloe is done. We should go."

We exited from the same door I'd come in, which,

unfortunately, was the only way in or out of the room. I preferred the separate exit at Red Moon. It was one thing to know people were out there; it was another thing to possibly see them.

But luckily whoever had been outside had disbanded before we emerged, most likely having already seen me wrap Sara in her robe. When we passed down the hall, we slipped behind other patrons, and I couldn't help but wonder, ***had they seen***?

THREE

Bennett Ryan

I couldn't decide if I felt fucking awesome—I'd basically just gotten my fiancée off in about three minutes in a back room of a swanky sex club—or more worked up and frustrated than I'd been in a long time. Fucking Chloe. The way she left made her little act feel like some sort of punishment for being in Vegas over Valentine's Day. But, shit, if I knew my fiancée at all, I knew that—no matter our role in the marketing world—she found the whole prospect of a manufactured romantic holiday completely ridiculous. Clearly she just jumped at the opportunity to play a little game and leave me in her favorite state: worked up and pissed off.

And fucking *Max*. Had he known Chloe was going to tease me like this? And, if he did . . . well, actually that was a little personal and creepy. I'd either have to kick his ass or drop something sleep-inducing into his drink and tattoo "I'm a wanker" in permanent ink all over his face.

But my revenge would have to wait. Max was gone when

I returned, and Henry and Will had the glassy-eyed look of two men given booze and women in heaping quantities.

"How goes it out here?" I asked, sitting back in my chair and picking up what I expected to be a mostly empty drink. Except, no. The drink was fresh, my plate of food refilled. I caught Gia's eyes across the room and raised my glass to her. For all of the mysterious corners and questionable sex acts behind closed doors, the staff was certainly on the job. She nodded to me, smiling, and then disappeared behind the bar. I couldn't help but notice that, in my time away, she'd removed everything else she wore and was now serving her tables completely nude.

I hoped for her sake it was a pleasant experience. It sounded a bit like one of my own recurring nightmares.

"How was the dancer?" Henry asked, still not bothering to look away from the stage. I probably could have lit his chair on fire and he wouldn't have noticed until the flames in his hair obstructed his view.

I studied him, trying to discern whether he was in on Chloe's surprise, but he didn't grin knowingly or even look all that interested in my answer. Will, too, only looked at me with bland curiosity.

"It was fine," I said.

"Quick," Will noted.

I grinned. Fuck yes, it was. I almost wished one of them *did* know about Chloe and her little stunt so I could at least get a high-five.

"There's some fucking amazing women here," Henry muttered. "I could watch this for the rest of the night."

Will stretched, checking his watch. "I'm starving, though. Don't we have dinner reservations? It's almost ten."

"Where's the Brit?" I asked, doing another survey of the giant room. It would be impossible to find him in here without checking each corner and bar.

"Don't know," Will said, shrugging and draining his scotch. "Disappeared right after you did."

Awareness tickled at the edge of my thoughts before understanding went off like a bomb: Sara was here, too. Chloe didn't answer when I asked whether she'd come here alone, but I couldn't imagine she came here solo just for this. Unless she planned to return to her hotel room to lounge in a bubble bath all night, she most definitely had other plans. If I'd been able to get a room alone with Chloe, no doubt Max was getting some time with his girlfriend somewhere as well.

After another drink and at least a handful of songs, Max returned to the table, approaching from behind us. I hadn't even seen him coming.

"Lads!" he proclaimed, clapping me on the back. "How are we enjoying all of the naked tits?"

We all murmured some variation of *"Great,"* and with a laugh that communicated how relaxed he was, Max lowered himself into the chair beside me.

"How was the dance, Ben?" he asked, eyes twinkling. "Not so bad after all, was it?"

I shrugged and took in his drunken smile. He looked about as relaxed as I was wound up. "You just got laid, didn't you, you fucking asshole?"

His eyes went wide and he leaned closer. "Didn't *you*?"

"Fuck no," I whispered, shaking my head, and Max burst out laughing. "She took care of herself, and then *left*."

He let out a low whistle and then sighed. "Guess you'll just have to catch up with her back home and give her some payback."

Was he serious? He expected me to let her go for the rest of the night—maybe even the rest of the long weekend—after doing something like that?

"Where are they headed?" I asked under my breath.

Max shrugged, scooping some caviar onto a blini from my plate. "Don't know, actually. Think they leave in the morning, though."

"Where are they staying?"

"Dunno. Sara took care of all of it." He seemed so much less concerned with all of this than I was . . . but of course he was. He clearly just got fucked in some room in the back while I only got to watch Chloe masturbate with my hand.

I glanced at the far wall just as Chloe and Sara stepped out from the black hallway, laughing together, arms linked. Max followed my attention and exhaled a deep breath. "Bloody hell they're lovely."

"Wonder where they're headed," I murmured.

Max looked over at me, already shaking his head as if he'd read my mind. "We've got a full night planned, mate."

"I'm sure we do."

"And they're doing their own thing."

"I'm sure they are."

He paused, watching as Sara caught his gaze and held it. Something passed from her eyes to his, something heavy and pleading. Behind her, Chloe looked up from where she'd been digging in her purse and saw me. Her lips parted and her hand fluttered up to her chest. In her eyes I could see genuine concern. Maybe even a touch of guilt. "You okay?" she mouthed.

If she felt guilty after her little act, then I was happy. I smirked. "No."

But any sign of guilt vanished as she smiled wickedly, blowing me a kiss and tugging Sara's arm. Together, Max and I watched them leave the club through the heavy steel doors we came through on entry.

"Fuck," Max whispered. "We're a couple of lucky arseholes."

I sighed. "Yeah."

I looked up and met his eyes. I knew he had a night planned, knew our activities were packed. But really, it was Friday night and we were here until Tuesday. Would it really matter if I slipped away for only an hour?

He leaned forward, grabbed my forearm, and started laughing. "Don't even fucking *think* about it, Bennett."

After the dim, almost cavelike atmosphere of the club, stepping outside was like being hit with a floodlight. Towering hotels crowded the dark sky and even from this distance, we could see the glow of LED and neon signs flashing from every casino on the strip. And *Christ,* was it loud. The sound of traffic blasted up from the street as we stood in the curved driveway in front of the building and waited for our driver. Cars stopped at the curb across the street, were emptied or loaded up before being driven away again. People of every shape and size shuffled by, horns honked in the distance, a series of sirens blared from a street a few blocks over.

And water *everywhere*—tinkling water features that filled the valet areas, the crashing sounds of waterfalls from the bigger hotels, and a massive fountain that nearly every tourist tossed coins into as they passed—even here, away from the glitz and glamour of the large casinos.

As if reading my mind, Henry walked over to a three-tiered fountain, peeking inside before skipping a poker chip across the rippling surface. "Who would have thought there'd be so much water in the desert?"

Will walked out behind us, taking off his coat even though it was cold out. "Water is a necessity of life," he said. "In order for a society to survive they need water to maintain its population. Such a seemingly cavalier and extravagant use of an important resource would illustrate that a community is thriving. A thriving populace makes people feel optimistic; an optimistic tourist spends more money and boosts the economy." He shrugged, placing a stick of chewing gum into his mouth. "Plus, it's just fucking pretty, you know?"

Henry gaped at him. "You really are a nerd."

"Isn't he, though?" Max said, smiling fondly.

Will lifted his chin toward Henry. "I'm not the one that just tossed a hundred-dollar chip into a fountain because it's what I've been conditioned to do. So thanks for proving my point."

Henry's eyes widened and he raced back to the edge of the water. "Son of a bitch."

Will leaned back against the brick façade, hands in his pocket and suit jacket tucked in the crook of his arm. "So how are we continuing this weekend of debauchery? Dinner and then what? Skydiving? Virgin sacrifice? Matching tattoos to commemorate the loss of Ben's balls?"

I smirked at him. Will had become a fixture in our lives ever since Max and Sara had reconciled. The five of us saw each other several times a week for lunches, dinners, and shows. Will was the designated bachelor of the group, and seemed to enjoy reminding us that Max and I were pussy-whipped non-men. "The thing you couldn't possibly understand, Will, is there is a benefit to fucking only one woman: she learns *exactly* what to do. I'm more than happy to give Chloe full access to my balls."

At this Henry stepped away from the fountain again and moved toward Will. "Besides, a hundred bucks says you couldn't even *find* a virgin in this place."

Will glanced down to Henry's waiting palm and laughed. "We've only been out of that club for two minutes and you've just thrown away a hundred-dollar poker chip *and* offered another hundred-dollar bet. I can't wait to see what you do in an actual casino."

"I win money," Henry said, pounding his chest with drunken machismo, before wincing.

I groaned, scrubbing my face with my hand. "I can't take you anywhere."

"You just got a lap dance, Benny," Henry said, shoving my shoulder. "How are you crabby? You should be smiling like a fool."

I turned in the direction of Max's laughter. "Ignore him," he told the others while motioning to me. "Our Ben's just feeling a bit frustrated is all."

Fucking Max. With his hands in his pockets and that dopey smile on his face, he was a portrait of nonchalance, and the exact opposite of everything I felt.

I could strangle Chloe right now—a feeling I'd grown increasingly familiar with since the day we met. All this time and she could *still* push my buttons like no other. To be honest, I wasn't entirely sure which of us was more fucked up: her for getting off on teasing me like this, or me for enjoying it so damn much.

"So . . . plans?" Will repeated, pushing away from the building. "Are we standing here all night watching Bennett throw a fit or. . . ?"

Max checked his watch. "Dinner," he said. "Mum made us reservations for the Steakhouse over at the Wynn. Supposed to be top-notch."

Looking for our driver, I turned to look down the street, and a flash of green caught my eye at the opposite corner. *Chloe.* I'd last seen her with Sara, all bright eyes and teasing smiles as she'd left me inside the club. Now they waited on the sidewalk, arms outstretched as they attempted to hail a cab.

I blinked quickly to Max, who was busy arguing with Will and Henry about whether it was physically possible to eat a twenty-four-ounce porterhouse in less than fifteen minutes. Perfect.

I spotted our car as it rounded the corner and began its way up the drive toward us, and realized I'd have to act quickly. With only the vaguest threads of a plan in place, I grimaced, hunching over and pressing a hand to my stomach.

"You okay over there, Ben?" Will asked, eyebrows raised.

"Fine, fine," I said, waving him off. "My stomach's just a little . . . I think my ulcer's acting up."

Max narrowed his eyes. "You have an ulcer?"

"Yes," I said, nodding, and sucking in breath for added effect.

"*You,*" he repeated. "An ulcer."

I straightened a little. "Is there a problem?"

He scratched his eyebrow and looked at me skeptically. "Suppose I'm just having a hard time wrapping my head around the idea that the great and powerful Bennett, the one whose blood-pressure barely blinks even in the most stressful meetings and has zero fucks to give about anyone's opinion"—he motioned between all three of them—"including ours," he added, "has an ulcer."

Our car pulled up to the curb in front of us just as a taxi stopped in front of Sara and Chloe.

"Well, I do," I said, meeting his stare again. Our driver opened the door and waited. *Everyone* waited, eyes moving from Max to me and back again.

"Why is this the first I'm hearing of this ulcer business?" Henry asked.

"Because you're not my doctor or my mommy," I said. They all stared at me in silence, looking various degrees of concerned or, in Max's case, doubtful. "Look, why don't you all take the car while I run to the pharmacy. I saw one just down the street."

Max continued to watch me over the car door. "Why don't you just come with us and we'll stop on the way?"

"Not necessary," I said, waving him off. "I'll have to call it in and I don't want anyone waiting on me. You guys go on ahead; I'll pick up my prescription and meet you at the restaurant."

"Fine by me," Henry said, and climbed into the car.

"We can wait," Will offered, though halfheartedly. It was clear everyone but Max was willing to let a man get some medicine for his damn ulcer.

"No, let him run along," Max said with a smirk. "I'm guessing poor Ben actually has a case of the trots and is afraid he's going to shit himself." He turned back at me. "We'll meet you at the restaurant."

I glared. He was lucky I didn't have time to argue. He was also lucky I didn't have time to walk over there and punch his smug face. "I'll meet you there."

I waited just long enough for the car to pull away before I turned, searching for a cab. The one Chloe and Sara were in had just reached the streetlight, and if I hurried, I could still catch up. When a car pulled over, I climbed in, promising the cabbie a small fortune if he could get me wherever they were going, and fast. I hadn't exactly worked out what I would do or how'd I'd get her alone, but I was operating on autopilot: get to Chloe, get her alone, get myself off.

My fiancée surprised me with a lap dance in a sex club and then I hopped in a cab for a car chase. My bachelor party in Vegas had officially begun.

Their cab stopped just down the Strip and I watched as they both climbed out. I paid my driver and stayed back, watching for a moment as they talked, each of them pointing in a different direction—Sara at Planet Hollywood and Chloe at the Cosmopolitan. When they appeared to reach a decision, they nodded, kissing each other's cheek before heading in opposite directions.

Fucking perfect.

Climbing out, I followed Chloe through the late-night crowds and into the building. The Cosmopolitan casino was dark and it took a moment for my eyes to adjust. Pinpoint colors, flashing lights, and the sound of electronic dings filled the air as I scanned the large room. I found her near the front of the casino, turning to climb a set of stairs.

Beads of sparkling crystals hung from the ceiling several stories up and curved around the giant staircase. From where I stood, it looked like Chloe was disappearing into a giant chandelier.

I followed, staying just far enough away to admire her ass as she moved, and wondering what exactly she was doing here. Was she meeting someone? Although she'd never mentioned any, maybe she had friends in Las Vegas. Or, perhaps she was simply waiting here for Sara to finish whatever she was doing across the street. My blood heated over the sheer *mystery* of Chloe; we lived together, worked together, and for all intents and purposes our lives were completely intertwined. But I relished knowing that she would always keep me guessing. Because of her wild independence, I would never know absolutely everything in her mind. Even when she was entirely *mine,* she would always be a challenge.

As we neared the third floor of the spiraling club, her destination grew no clearer to me, and the wickedness of her little game started to bloom into an ache in my abdomen. I gave in, hungry to fall into the familiar routine of chastising her, and then having my way with her body. In only a few long strides I was there, wrapping my hand around her upper arm.

"You are in so much trouble," I growled into her hair.

I felt her stiffen for a moment before going lax, the tension slipping from her body as she leaned back against my chest.

"I wondered how long it would take you to find me."

"*You,*" I said as we continued climbing the spiraling staircase, "have done enough talking for tonight." We were fully inside the glimmering, beaded curtains now, and they seemed to wrap all around us, twinkling in the soft light. "It's time for you to keep that pretty little mouth closed . . . unless I have need for it."

We reached the third story, where a rather impressive bar was situated, the shelves lined in jewel-colored bottles and draped in even more of the sparkling gems. Continuing on, I led us to a darkened corner. Smiling, I noticed the sign above a door tucked into the corner: I needed to be alone with Chloe on my terms and, quite frankly, we'd always been pretty great in restrooms.

An older gentleman with dyed black hair looked up in surprise as we entered the men's room. I reached out to shake his hand, and pressed a folded bill into his palm.

"It's so noisy out there," I said, nodding in the direction of the casino and bar on the other side of the door. "Perhaps you'd be good enough to give us a few minutes to talk?"

He looked down at the money, his eyes widening, and then smiled back up at me. "'Talk'?"

"Yes, sir."

His gaze moved to Chloe. "That okay with you, miss? I might not look like much now, but back in my day I could drop a pretty boy like this before he knew what hit him."

Beside me, Chloe laughed. "Something tells me you still could," she said with a wink. "And trust me, I'm perfectly capable of dropping this pretty boy as well."

"I don't doubt that." His smile widened, revealing a white, toothy grin. "You know," he said, looking down at his watch, "I just realized it's time I took my break." He reached for a hat hanging on a hook and set it on his head, winking as he moved the CLOSED FOR CLEANING sign outside and in front of the door.

I watched her for a moment as the door shut behind him, then crossed the room to flip the lock.

Chloe lifted herself up to the wide marble counter and sat looking at me, long legs crossed in front of her. The room was luxurious, more of a sitting room with adjoining stalls than a traditional bathroom. The floor was the same black and gold as the rest of the casino, with three wing-back chairs grouped against the far wall and a blue leather bench set between them. A huge, tinkling chandelier hung in the center of the room, painting the walls in specks of colored light.

"Am I in trouble?" she asked, eyes hopeful.

"A world of trouble." I took a step toward her.

"This seems to be a reoccurring theme."

"Doesn't it?"

"Are you going to tell me what I did wrong?" She looked up at me with wide eyes and cheeks a mischievous pink. She was so fucking beautiful. "Should I have used my own hand instead?"

"Not funny." My heart slammed beneath my ribs, and I grew drunk from the steady thrum of adrenaline as it slipped through my veins. Her gaze never wavered as I crossed the room to spread her legs and step between her thighs.

I trailed a finger down the smooth skin of her calf, wrapping a hand around her ankle. "These shoes don't look very sensible," I said, brushing a thumb over the soft leather.

She continued to watch me, lips red and slick and so fucking tempting. "Maybe I'm not feeling very sensible this weekend. Is that why I'm in trouble?"

"You're in trouble because you're impossible."

She lifted her chin and met my eyes. "I learned from the best."

I moved her foot to my hip and traced a path up her thigh and beneath her skirt. I clenched my jaw as a fresh wave of frustration swept through me over how she'd left me at the club, how proud she was for leaving me hard, and how ninety percent of our arguments could be boiled down to one of us trying to get a reaction out of the other. Seriously fucked-up situation we had going on here.

Still.

Gripping her ass with both hands, I ignored her sharp inhale as I jerked her to the edge of the counter.

"You—" She started to protest, but I stopped her, placing a finger against her mouth. She still smelled unfamiliar—floral, not citrus—but beneath the heavy makeup and new perfume there was something softer in her eyes, something inherently Chloe. She could play dress-up all she wanted, but the woman who was mine would always be there. The realization was like drowning, and I leaned forward, replacing my finger with my lips and quickly becoming lost in her little breaths and sounds as she moved eagerly into my touch. Her kiss felt like a drug seeping into my bloodstream, and I pushed my hand into her hair and tilted her head, wanting more than the soft flicks of tongue between our parted lips.

With my palm on her chest, I guided her to lie down onto the counter, moving her how I wanted and not being particularly gentle about it, either. But she went willingly, eyes widening in recognition of the game we were playing, mouth soft and open. She leaned back on her elbows and looked up at me, waiting to see what I'd do next.

The gauzy material of her skirt felt like nothing in my hands as I slid it up her hips, exposing miles of leg and a different pair of satin panties beneath. I let my fingers press into her skin, wanting to hold her down and mark her up, hear her beg for what she wanted.

"I'm going to fuck you with my mouth," I said, kneeling between her thighs and ghosting my lips over the thin material. "Fuck you with my tongue until you're begging for my cock. Maybe I'll give it to you." I shrugged. "Maybe I won't."

She sucked in a short breath and reached for my hair, trying to pull me forward. "Don't tease, Bennett," she said.

I pushed her hands away, laughing as I looked up at her. "You don't get to make any of the decisions tonight, Chloe. Not after your bullshit game in the club." I breathed again where her legs parted, flicking my tongue over her clit until the fabric of her panties was thick with wetness. "You kissed me, let me taste your tits, *came on my hand,* and then left me there. Hard. That wasn't very nice."

"I . . . what?" she said, eyes unfocused as she watched me, a flush of color moving up her neck.

Leaning forward again, I pinned her hips to the counter, kissing and nipping at her through the thin satin until it was soaked. Her head fell back and she moaned, whispering my name into the silent room.

"Louder," I said against her. "Let me hear you."

"Take them off. Suck on me."

The neediness in her voice sent a jolt of electricity through my body and I wrapped the thin straps in my hand and viciously ripped them, wanting them down and gone and nothing between her and my mouth.

She cried out, arching against me at the first touch of my tongue to her skin, her fingers digging into my hair and her voice ringing all around us.

The space was awkward but it didn't matter, and was more than made up for when I looked to the side to find her watching our reflection in the mirror, teeth biting into her bottom lip. I met her eyes as I tasted her, sliding my tongue across and inside.

I added a finger, then two, and watched as they moved in her, wet with how much she wanted me. Her voice was nothing more than a breathy whisper and my name over and over as she asked for more and opened her legs wider, the heel of her sexy shoe scraping along the countertop. I could feel the heat of her all around me, the way she started to tremble as she got closer.

"Good?" I asked, making sure my voice vibrated against her.

She nodded, breathless, moving her hands above her head to push into her hair. "So good. Oh fuck, Bennett, so close."

God it was torture, wanting to watch her lose control, but wanting to *feel* it, too, *needing* to feel her.

I tried to hide my desperation as I fit my hands to her hips and all but threw her to the bench, hovering above her to lick a line from her navel to the scrap of lace she called a bra. Sitting up, I unbuttoned the top of my shirt, reached blindly for my belt, and undid my pants. I freed my cock and almost gasped as she swatted my hand away and took me in her palm.

"No," I said, flipping her over to her knees and stepping behind her. "You had your time to play earlier. This is mine." I lifted her ass into the air, slapping it hard.

She gasped, turning around to look at me.

I gave her a dark smile, running my hand over her skin, soothing. "Do you want me to stop?"

Her eyes narrowed into a glare.

"You are welcome to stop me anytime," I murmured. "I'm sure this is absolute torture for you."

I brushed the tip of my cock through her wetness and down to her clit, circling, teasing.

"You're an asshole," she managed finally, and I brought my hand against her ass again, harder. But this time instead of surprise, she moaned, hoarse and hungry.

Then that was all there was: Chloe and the sounds she made, the way she asked me to push inside, to fuck her. And when I did, and smacked her ass again, she pleaded for *harder* and *more.*

But even when I took what I wanted it wasn't enough; it never would be. I could feel the weight of it somewhere deep in my stomach—the absolute love I felt for her, the constant need to touch and feel and take, to mark her from the inside out.

I twisted my fingers in the material of her shirt, pulled it lower so I could see her breasts move as I fucked her. Her hair fell across her back and I ran my hands under it, feeling the cool strands against my skin. I watched as I slid in and out of her, the way she pushed back against me, her skirt bunched up over her pink ass and around her hips.

"I miss this," I said, covering the mark I'd made, pressing down on it. "All the time."

She nodded, said my name. I could hear the frustration in her voice as she reached for something to hold on to, her other hand moving down between her legs.

"That's right," I said, watching her touch herself. "Get there. Make yourself come."

It must have been what she needed because she cried out, spine arching as she pushed back against me. I was close, could barely think and so fucking hungry for it I could hardly breathe. My legs burned, muscles protesting as I thrust into her over and over. The legs of the bench scraped against the stone floor; the leather creaked beneath us.

"Bennett. Fuck, *Bennett*," she said, and heat pooled low in my stomach, building and building until it was pulsing through me, my vision going dark and fuzzy around the edges as I came.

Every part of me seemed to give out at once as I collapsed, panting and exhausted, gripping the bench for support.

"Holy shit." The room was spinning and so quiet that my voice and even our breathing seemed to echo off the marble. I wondered how loud we'd been.

She stood, wobbling the slightest bit as she straightened her clothes and moved to a stall to clean herself up. "You know I have to walk around after this?"

I grinned. "Of course."

"You did that on purpose."

I rolled to my back and blinked up to the sparkling chandelier. "At least I let you come, too."

I knew I should straighten my clothes and find the boys, but right now all I wanted to do was sleep.

She moved to stand over me, leaning down to press a soft, lingering kiss to my mouth. "You need to go get some dinner or you'll be drunk by midnight."

I groaned, trying to pull her down to me, but she escaped by shoving her finger between my ribs. "Ow! Isn't that the point?"

"I'm sure they're wondering where you are."

"I told them I had an ulcer to get them to go on without me."

"And they believed you?"

I shrugged. "Who the fuck knows."

"Well, go convince them that you've recovered from your completely unbelievable illness and I'm going to meet Sara."

"Fine," I said, standing to pull up my pants. I watched as she leaned forward, smoothing out her hair in the mirror. "Where *is* Sara?"

"She's meeting up with a friend who lives here. A dancer, I think? Some sort of cabaret or stripper thing at Planet Hollywood."

"Now that sounds interesting," I said.

She met my reflection with raised brows before continuing. "Anyway, I had a feeling I was being stalked and told her to go on without me."

"A feeling?"

She shrugged, applying her lipstick. "A hope."

Snapping the cap back on her makeup, she closed it up in her purse and I followed her to the door, lifting a hand to her face. "I love you anyway," I said.

"I love you anyway, too," she said, leaning in to kiss me before slapping my ass, *hard*.

I could still hear her laughter long after she disappeared through the door.

Four

Max Stella

I watched out the rear window as Bennett's long, purposeful strides carried him down the sidewalk. He looked back over his shoulder and hailed a taxi as soon as he thought we were out of sight.

Bloody hell. For someone known for being so absolutely unflappable, he was a mess. He hadn't even kept up that flimsy charade of an illness long enough to see us down the end of the street and 'round the corner.

I turned back in my seat, watching as the lights and tourists roaming the sidewalks passed by in a blur, and let my thoughts move to Sara. She'd said she felt hollow with how much she wanted me, and *Christ,* just the memory of those words was enough to wreck me all over again. She was so rarely demanding, and even during our busiest weeks when we hardly saw each other, she was the patient one out of the two of us, always insisting we'd make up for lost time on the weekend, or on a Wednesday. For her to tell me she needed more tonight made it almost impossible to deny her. But I could see, in her eyes, the way she'd immediately regretted it, as if by telling me that she knew I'd be torn.

With her eerie sense of timing, my phone buzzed with a text from her: I'm fine, honestly. I'm sorry I distracted you.

I smiled as I typed my reply: Alas, you're my favorite distraction.

Have fun with the boys tonight, she wrote back.

A loud pop drew my attention and I blinked over to where Henry and Will had uncorked a bottle of champagne. "Show of hands for those of us who think Bennett just needed to rub one out in the bathroom," Will said, offering me a glass of champagne. I waved it off, waiting instead for a real drink at the restaurant.

"We did just leave a strip club," Henry said, protective-brother mode in full force. "Cut the man some slack."

I worked to keep my expression neutral. Will and Henry didn't know the girls were here, but they were eerily close to the mark.

"Henry's right," I cut in, surprised to find myself defending Bennett for deserting us to go shag his fiancée during the first night of his *stag* weekend. "Maybe he just needed a moment. The man is notoriously ruled by his dick."

"Ha!" Will barked. "I love the implication that you're any different."

It didn't matter that he was right, and since meeting Sara I'd thought of practically nothing else beyond what she was doing, what she was wearing, and of course, where I could fuck her. The side of me that loved to argue with Will couldn't resist responding. "I'll admit that Sara takes up a great deal of my thoughts—" I began.

"Understandable," Will interrupted, giving me a knowing glance.

"*But,*" I continued, ignoring him, "I'm perfectly capable of keeping my head in the game when necessary."

Unfazed, he hummed and topped off his drink, settling back into the supple leather seat. "Yes. Clear-headed businessman like yourself, never dream of shirking responsibility or, let's say . . . friendship, for a woman."

I nodded warily, sensing a trap.

"And when you missed picking me up after my flight back from China because you had an 'emergency,'" he said, using air quotes, "which of course means getting sucked off by Sara in the back of your car in the airport parking lot, that was keeping your head in the game."

I felt the weight of Henry's congratulatory slap across my back. "You sly son of a bitch," he said.

I winked at Henry, knowing Will was far from done.

"And when you ditched me with three of the most boring clients on the planet for two hours because you were fucking Sara in the library at James's house—that *also* was keeping your head in the game. Yeah, Ryan could really take a lesson and stop thinking with his cock."

"I think you've got it about squared," I said, laughing.

"Just making sure," he said with a charming smile, lifting his champagne flute to his forehead in salute.

We stopped at a light just beyond the Palazzo and although I was looking forward to the meal, I wished I'd had the idea to run to the "pharmacy" before Bennett did.

"See, if you kept a better schedule," Will continued, "you wouldn't be so desperate to *shag* whenever you get a free second."

"Schedule?" Henry asked.

I sat forward, smiling. "He means his calendar of women. Our Will here might not be attached or fucking everything in a skirt, but he's certainly never at a loss for company. He keeps his 'relationships' neat and tidy and in regular rotation on his calendar."

Will frowned while Henry looked between us, obviously confused, and asked, "Wait. Are you telling me you schedule your booty calls?"

"No," Will answered, glaring in my direction. "It means the women I'm involved with each know about the other. They also know I'm not interested in anything more for the time being, which works perfectly because neither are they. Everyone gets what they want." He threw his hands up and shrugged. "You won't find me running to the pharmacy, or banging a girl in the middle of a work meeting because I can't find any other time in my schedule."

"Right . . ." Henry and I said in unison.

The car jolted to a stop and we each moved to a window. "Looks like we're finally here," Will said. "Jesus, what took so long?"

The door opened and we climbed out in front of the Wynn, taking in the scene around us. It was chaos. Rows of cars lined the curb, many of them still running and with the doors left open. Handfuls of bewildered attendants stood around in small groups, obviously at a loss for what to do.

"Looks like there's a broken hydrant on the property," our driver said, motioning over his shoulder. "I can drop you off but it'll be at least an hour before I'd be able to get back in to pick you up."

The other two rounded the car to join us and I sighed, looking down to my watch. "Shouldn't be a problem," I said. "We're having dinner and something tells me it's not going to be quick." I was torn between wanting a night out with my best mates, and wanting to make sure Sara was sorted. I was growing more wound up, feeling restless and edgy despite the time I'd spent with her just an hour ago.

The driver nodded and we left him at the curb, moving inside and deeper into the casino, following the signs until we'd reached the restaurant. There was a club nearby and the persistent thump of music could be felt through the walls, through the floor, as we crossed the sleek restaurant and each took a seat at our table. The pulsing music mirrored the tension building in my limbs, the rhythmic beat of *Sara Sara Sara* humming beneath my skin.

I checked my mobile for the hundredth time and frowned when I saw there were no further messages. Where was she? Had Bennett found Chloe and if so, why hadn't Sara texted yet?

I thumbed through a few of the more recent photos on my phone: the two of us curled up in my bed; a photo of her spread below me, limbs heavy with satisfaction after a good, hard fuck; a close-up of her naked breasts; my hand on her ass as I took her from behind late at night in my office.

I realized I'd lost the thread of the conversation when Will's voice broke into my haze, from studying a photo of Sara's red, red lips around my cock.

"Max." Will rapped his knuckles on the table.

I looked up, surprised to find our waiter standing at the table, and quickly turned off my screen.

"Something to drink, sir?"

"Sorry," I murmured. "Macallan, neat."

"Twelve, eighteen, or twenty-one years, sir?"

My eyes went wide. "Twenty-one. *Brilliant.*"

After jotting it down he stepped away, and I attempted to go back to my phone, only to be interrupted by Will again. "Share with the class or put that thing away. I know what you have on there, you sick bastard. No girls, remember?"

Henry nodded as he tossed a piece of bread at me from across the table. "Dudes only," he agreed.

Will leaned forward, reminding me, "The promise of not being a third wheel with you was the only reason I let you talk me into this in the first place."

I sighed and tucked my phone away, knowing he was right. When I looked up my eyes widened, catching the path of Bennett as he walked through the restaurant to join us.

"Well, well. Look who it is," I said.

Henry pulled the chair out for his brother. "Feeling better?"

Bennett unbuttoned his suit jacket and took a seat. "Much," he said, grinning.

Bennett Ryan was fucking *grinning*.

Our drinks arrived and I reached for mine, looking at him over the rim of my glass. "Didn't take too long, either, did it?" I asked, feeling a satisfied thrill when his expression fell just long enough to glare at me. "Some things are better when they're fast. Like a *pharmacy.*"

"Nothing like efficiency to make a man happy," he agreed with a self-satisfied grin.

"And you're a king among men," I said, laughing and holding my glass up for him to toast with his water. "Get yourself a cocktail in celebration of efficient pharmacies everywhere."

"Why do I feel like I'm only getting half this conversation?" Will asked, looking dumbly between us. His eyes narrowed. "Is something going on we don't know about?"

I barked out a laugh. "Don't know what you're on about, mate. Just taking the piss."

Henry began studying the menu but Will seemed less convinced, looking away only when Henry called his attention to a cart of flaming meat being rolled by our table.

Satisfied they were sufficiently distracted, I leaned toward Bennett. "Where's Sara?"

"Wouldn't you love to know?"

I narrowed my eyes at him, scowling. "Arsehole."

"Hey, you started this," Bennett said, reaching for my drink.

I smacked his hand away. "Me? What are you on about?"

"You know: Chloe? Here? As grateful as I am, don't

try and pretend it wasn't you who suggested the whole lap dance thing."

"For *you.*"

"For me," he said, smirking. "Right. So I'd be distracted and you could be with Sara in that club."

Maybe he had a point.

"You can't tell me if Sara teased you for forty-five minutes in a strip club you wouldn't immediately go find her and . . . fix things. Even if you were meant to be hanging out with the guys."

I laughed. "Too right." I leaned closer, voice low. The idea of being able to slip out of here and have Sara one more time was too delicious to pass up. "This dinner is going to take at least two hours. I could be back in twenty."

This time when he reached for my drink, I let him take it. "She's visiting a friend," he whispered.

I paused. "Visiting . . . what?"

"Oh, that bothers you? Leaves you feeling unresolved? I'm not so sure I should tell you," he said, studying me. "It's pretty clear the start of this night has gone far better for you than for me. Maybe your focus should be on my bachelor party instead of what's in your pants."

"Or," I began, "I could tell Henry about that time you shagged two girls in his bed when he was stuck working at school over the uni holidays."

That sobered him up. "She has a friend that dances in some show at Planet Hollywood. Chloe mentioned something about Sara going over there for sound check or something between performances."

Sara, sitting in a dark theater all alone? That was all I needed to hear. Pushing away from the table, I stood. Will and Henry looked up at me from their menus. "Where are you going?" Henry asked. "They have a forty-ounce rib eye!"

"Toilet," I said, placing a hand over my stomach. "I'm, ah . . . not feeling well."

"You, too?" Will asked.

I nodded, hesitating for only a moment before saying, "Back in a bit."

And I was off, sprinting from the restaurant, blood pumping hot in my legs and that untethered need to be with her buzzing steadily under my skin.

The smell of asphalt hit me in the face as I raced down to the curb, looking up the distance to Planet Hollywood on my phone as I walked. This was shite. It was several blocks away, and at this point in the night the streets were packed with slow-walking tourists looking and pointing at every possible sight between here and where I would find Sara.

Although the car traffic on Las Vegas Boulevard had cleared up significantly, the valet area was still a mess: some of the same cars were parked curbside and there wasn't a taxi in sight. *Fuck,* how was I going to get there? I looked down into the car next to me: door still open, Eiffel Tower key chain hanging from the ignition.

The keys were *swinging*, as if they were actually trying to grab my attention.

It took me all of five seconds to decide that I'd lived my entire life without stealing a car, and how could I possibly have let that happen?

Borrowing, I thought. I was borrowing.

With a quick look 'round, I slipped in through the open door and turned the key. A dark hat sat on the leather seat next to me and I picked it up, turning it over once before placing it on my head. *Oh well, when in Rome and all that.*

I had no idea what in the actual hell I was doing as I raced away from the curb, but I rationed that at this point, nothing else could possibly go wrong.

It turned out that driving a stolen—*borrowed*—limousine was every bit as difficult as one might imagine. It was awkward and handled like shit, and wasn't exactly the most inconspicuous thing on the road. But traffic was almost nonexistent and soon I was arriving at the blazing neon casino.

With my fingers crossed I pulled into the underground parking garage, tossing my hat and the keys to the first valet attendant I saw. Borrowing a stranger's car during a stag party in Vegas . . . another tick off the bucket list.

I was met with a bank of escalators as I stepped inside, declining the opportunity to stand still and take a breather, opting instead to race up them two at a time. Rows of purple neon were embedded into the ceiling overhead, as well as a giant sparkling chandelier. I followed the signs to the opposite end of the casino, stopping just in front of the Peepshow theater.

I was stopped by an older lady at the ticket counter, who stood up to stop me from entering, insisting access pre-show was limited to performers and crew, only.

Taking a few seconds to study her—blonde hair with solid gray roots, heavy makeup and a bright red sequined top—I decided "Marilyn," as her name tag suggested I call her, had probably seen her share of loser men chasing after the showgirls here.

"A girl here, one of the performers, called tonight to tell me she's pregnant with my child. She told me she'd be here."

Marilyn's eyes grew to roughly the size of dinner plates. "I don't have your name on any list."

"Because it's personal, you see."

She nodded, obviously wavering.

I decided to close the deal. "I'm just here to make

sure she's okay." I had a momentary pang of guilt over the lie, but then I remembered Sara, in the dark theatre, alone. "I need to know if she needs money."

Once inside the darkened auditorium, I looked around. The stage lights overhead washed everything in more purple—the plush carpet, the seats, even the handful of people moving about on the stage. It was quiet and obviously in between shows, and there was just enough light for me to find Sara on the second level and begin making my way toward her. I climbed down slowly, taking the time to observe her as she sat, unaware. She was watching someone and smiling. She still took my breath away, and here, painted in violet light, I wanted to memorize everything about her: the shine of her hair, the smoothness of her skin. I wanted a picture of her, just like this.

As rehearsal started, the music began to swell, the lights dimming further as I descended the final rows to take a seat next to her. I could barely see my own hand in front of my face, but as if she'd known I was there all along—or maybe hoped I would find her—she hardly reacted. A simple glance, a small smile, and the tiny gold pendant I'd given her for Christmas twisting slowly between her delicate fingertips. I placed a hand on her thigh, felt the warm, supple skin beneath my palm, and motioned silently up to the stage.

A man counted down as girls in skimpy jeweled costumes balanced on pointed toes and spun themselves around. I was dizzy just watching them. They danced, circling one another and finally stopping beneath a concentrated beam of light, to kiss.

I tightened my grip on her thigh, swiped my thumb beneath the hem of her skirt, and heard the slight hitch in her breath. There was no one but us in the darkness beyond the stage and I wondered, would Sara's love for being watched translate into watching someone else?

My hand traveled farther up her thigh and I leaned in to kiss her ear. She sighed, tilting her head as I moved her hair, and traced my tongue down the curve of her neck.

She pulled back just enough to meet my eyes, letting hers flicker quickly to the performers in wordless communication. *Here?* she was asking. *While they dance and touch each other on stage?*

Another woman spun around a gold pole, the single spotlight accentuating every acrobatic movement of her graceful arms and legs, the way her body bowed to the pulse of the music that played in the background. It was erotic, and I felt myself harden even further both from the show in front of us and Sara's reaction to it.

I smiled, shifted in my seat to whisper against her cheek. "What are you thinking?" I asked.

"You have to ask?"

"Maybe I want to hear you say it," I said.

She swallowed. "Are we going to?" There was need in her voice. The edge of that hollow little ache I'd heard earlier at the Black Heart.

"Maybe not *everything*, Petal," I said, letting my fingers trail higher, pushing the lace of her pants to the side so I could run a finger along the soft folds of her pussy. "Are you still wet from me?"

She swallowed, flicked her tongue out to lick her lips. "Yes."

I dipped my finger inside. "Do you feel like you were fucked earlier? Can you still feel me?" I pressed deeper and she hiccupped the tiniest breath; her mouth went soft and round, glistening in the dim light.

"Someone might see us," she murmured, head falling back against the seat and eyes fluttering closed. She struggled to find words as I added a second finger, pushing them both in at once. I smiled at how breathless she was, how immediately incoherent.

"Isn't that the point?"

"Cameras . . ."

I glanced up and shrugged. "And what would you do, sweet Sara? If someone saw you this way? Would that make it better? Would you come on my hand as soon as you heard their feet on the stairs?"

She moaned quietly and I couldn't look away from the hint of movement between her thighs where I touched her, the way she spread her legs farther to open herself up, arching into it. I liked her pliant for me, boneless, where I could arrange her the way I wanted and just take. But I liked her like this, too, desperate and forgetting herself.

I groaned, squeezing myself through my trousers because—*Christ*—would it always be like this? Would I always want her in this way that made me dizzy and completely stupid?

I wanted to put her on my lap and ride up into her, hear her screams and the way she said my name over and over, hear it echo off the high ceilings, echoed above the music. It would ring around us, sound back to me, and the people still dancing on the stage would know that she was mine.

Of course we couldn't, and when a small moan left her lips I leaned in, whispered a soft "Shhh," against her skin. Her eyes were pinned to the stage, where a woman danced topless, and in the almost pitch-black auditorium I struggled to make out the side of Sara's face. The rustle of fabric dragged my attention lower, to where she played with her breast, tugging on her nipple where her shirt had fallen open the tiniest bit. And the fact that she was getting off on what we were doing and where—by being watched but also watching in return—well, the thought alone was enough to get me riled up, have me almost shooting in my pants.

My heart kicked at my ribs and I palmed my cock,

watching, hearing as Sara got closer and closer. In the glow of the stage lights I could see a thin sheen of sweat across her forehead, could feel her beginning to tighten around my fingers. Her sounds changed, growing longer with every circle of my thumb over her clit, every rhythmic rock of her hips.

I could feel my orgasm building in my spine. "Sara," I said, but she leaned forward, catching my mouth in a rough kiss. I wished I had my phone out, or a camera set to record the way her teeth pulled at my lips, the way it must look when her tongue darted out to taste me.

Her breath hitched and I felt her body tense, felt her orgasm race through her, hot and wild, her sounds swallowed by the thump and bass of the music. She reached across me to fumble with my zipper and I was right behind her.

"Oh fuck yes," I said, practically melting into my seat. My head fell back and I gave myself over to the feeling. "Fuck, Petal, pull it hard. Fast."

Three rough strokes in and I felt the pleasure climb up my back, sparking light behind my eyelids and I came, pulsing in Sara's hand.

The music was suddenly deafening and I opened my eyes, feeling heat slip from my cock to finally return to the rest of my body. I blinked several times and was met with Sara's wide grin, the pleased expression she always wore when she'd proven once again how completely she owned me.

"There's one to add to the list," I said, focusing again on the performers still wandering around onstage. I saw her bend forward to reach for something in her purse, pulling out a tissue to wipe off her hands before dabbing at my trousers. "I suppose we're back to the old days? Where you tell me this is where it ends and I'm to zip myself up and leave you here."

Sara laughed. "How'd you manage to get away from them anyway?"

"Told them I was going to the toilet and left."

Her eyebrows disappeared beneath her hair and she fell back against the seat in laughter. "And you've been gone all this time?"

I nodded. "Suppose they'll try and suss out the truth of where I've gone. Damn them." I finished adjusting my clothes and leaned across the chair, taking her face in my hands and dragging a finger down her nose. "I've got to go."

"Yes, you do."

"I love you, Petal."

"Love you too, stranger."

FIVE

Bennett Ryan

I was pretty sure I looked like an idiot. Will and Henry continued to sip their drinks and pore over the menu, oblivious to the fact that I was sitting across from them, damn near giggling and randomly breaking into the widest, goofiest grins imaginable.

Despite Max's sudden departure, I was still on a high from how much fun it had been to follow Chloe, then spank and fuck her in a bathroom. And she was going to be my wife.

I had no idea how I'd gotten so lucky.

"Are you gentlemen ready?" the waiter asked, removing a slew of empty glasses from the table and stacking them on his tray. Will and Henry looked up for the first time in about ten minutes and blinked around the table.

"Max not back yet?" Will asked, surprised.

I shook my head, refolding my napkin in an attempt to avoid their eyes. "Doesn't look like it."

"Should we wait for him or. . . ?" Henry asked. "I could

go out and kill a few minutes at one of the tables while we wait."

I glanced down at my watch and groaned; the flimsy excuse Max had used about needing the bathroom was most definitely losing its credibility with each passing minute. And it wasn't that I particularly cared if Max got busted—it's possible that might actually improve my night—but if Max went down then so did I. We had the rest of the weekend with these guys, and Will would make it a living hell if he found out we'd been sneaking out to bang our girlfriends on Valentine's Day.

And, truth be told, Will was the only single one here and was the most focused on hanging out with the guys. I felt a pang of guilt that, of the three of us who seemed to care more for women than gambling, he was the only one *not* getting laid this weekend.

"Sure he'll be back any minute," I said. "Must not have been feeling well."

"What the hell did you two eat anyway?" Henry asked.

I tried to formulate an answer and remembered the waiter only when I heard him sigh. "I'll give you gentlemen a few more minutes," he said before stepping away.

Will narrowed his eyes. "Yeah, what *is* going on," he said, words slurring together a little. "There's no way a person could have this much diarrhea and survive."

"Thank you for that very tasteful analysis." I set my napkin on my plate and stood. "I'll just step over there and see how much longer. You two go ahead and order for us. I'll have the filet. Bloody." I started to walk away and stopped, turning to face them again. "Oh, and get yourself a few more drinks," I added with a smile. "It's on me."

The mood in the restaurant had changed as the night went on. Lights embedded in the ceiling and around the room had shifted from the soft white to warm gold, washing everything in rich color. The music was louder, not so loud that you couldn't talk or make out individual conversations, but loud enough that you could feel it deep in your chest, a pounding like a second heartbeat. It felt more like a nightclub than a restaurant now and made it easier for me to step out unnoticed, to text Max.

Where the fuck are you?

I paced the glossy wood floors just outside, debating whether I could leave and get away with it. My phone vibrated with his incoming message less than a minute later.

Just pulling up. Two minutes.

We need to talk, I answered. *I'll meet you near valet.*

With a glance over my shoulder to make sure Will or Henry hadn't followed, I headed down to meet Max.

The casino floor was bustling. The sound of laughter and cheering floated up from one of the tables and a couple of police officers stood near the entrance, speaking to a group of valets.

Max stepped through the doors and stopped just in front of me, rebuttoning his suit jacket and straightening his tie.

"Always so impatient," he said, glancing twice at the police before gripping my arm. "Perhaps we could move just over here . . ." He guided us away from the area and out of their direct line of sight.

"Oh, that's comforting. You're dodging the police now? Jesus Christ, what is happening? I feel like an accomplice in some sort of crime spree," I said, running a hand through my hair.

"The less you know, the better, mate. Trust me."

"And the toilet, Max? Really? That's the best you could come up with?"

"As if your excuse was any better? An ulcer? You've lost your touch, mate. The Ben I knew in uni would be ashamed. Love's made you soft."

I sighed, glancing behind me. "You've been gone for almost an hour. What the fuck took you so long?"

He gave me a wide, leering smile. He looked happy. Fuck, he looked downright giddy, as if he hadn't a care in the world. I knew that expression; I'd been wearing it less than ten minutes ago.

"Just gave the lady friend a screaming orgasm, mate."

"Okay, right. I did not need to know that."

"You're one to talk." He stretched his neck, cracking it. "So how are the boys?"

"Replacing most of their blood with vodka and discussing the beauty of aged meats."

"Shall we head up for dinner, then?"

He went to push by me but I reached for his arm, stopping him. "Look, you know what I've been doing and I know what you've been doing, let's cut the bullshit. Back in New York, I'm lucky to get Chloe to myself for ten full minutes. They're only here tonight. Let's help each other out here."

His expression seemed to sober and he nodded. "Am I the only one that finds it hilarious that it's Valentine's Day and *we're* the ones behaving like idiots and chasing them rather than the other way 'round?"

"The thought may have occurred to me once or twice, yes," I said with a shake of my head. These women made us insane. "We need a plan. It will be no problem to get our comrades lost in a meat coma but that won't last all night. And Will is getting suspicious."

"Agreed," he said. "How much do you think he knows?"

"I'm not sure. Henry hasn't stopped drinking or looking at the poker chips in his pocket all night, but Will—he seems to be under the impression that you and I are both suffering from some sort of horrible digestive issue."

Max groaned. "I'll want to see her again, mate. I have to be honest. She's here, and she's . . . well, I'd like to check in on her again." He looked up at me and I nodded, understanding. "Will would never let me live it down if he thinks I couldn't go a single weekend without seeing her. You *know* him. I love the man but he's enough of a tosser as it is; I'm not giving him this, too," he said, shaking his head.

"Exactly. My brother loves giving me shit about Chloe and the fact that I slept with her while she still worked for me. If he finds out about this there won't be a Ryan family holiday where he doesn't regale everyone with the story of *the other time Bennett couldn't keep it in his pants*. Fuck that."

"Right."

"So what now? If we wanted to see them again tonight, how could that work?"

Max paced back and forth in front of the registration desk before turning to face me. "I think I've got it."

"Tell me."

"I'm thinking . . ." He was looking down at the ground, still putting the pieces together in his head. "I think . . . we need them distracted, yeah? And we want to make sure Will has a brilliant night."

I nodded. "But it's got to be more than booze. Those two have been drinking all night and somehow still seem to be functioning. I don't want them blind or facedown in a gutter somewhere."

"Obviously." Max pulled out his phone and began scrolling through the contacts. I shifted from foot to foot and kept glancing over my shoulder, waiting for Henry to come out and drag me back by my collar to the table.

When I turned back to Max, he'd stopped on a number. "Who are you calling?"

"Mr. Johnny French," he said.

"How do you know him, anyway? An old friend?"

Max laughed. "Not sure I'd call him a friend. Not sure he'd call *anyone* a friend, really. But he does owe me a few favors and as you've seen, caters to the type of crowd that might be helpful in our situation."

"I'm afraid to see where this is going."

"A little faith, mate. Will is a bit of a ladies' man," he said, smiling. "We'll just . . . help him."

"Help him?"

Max shrugged, meaningfully.

"You mean get him a *hooker*?" I practically shouted.

Max shushed me and glanced around. "A little louder perhaps? And who'd have thought you'd be such a prude, Ben? I'm a little surprised," he said. "I'm not going to let him sleep with her. We just want a *distraction*. We're getting him a distraction."

"But—"

He held up a finger to silence me, and put the phone on speaker between us. It rang a few times before it was answered by a man with a deep, serious voice: Johnny French.

"What can I do for you, Max? Again," he said.

"How are you this evening, Mr. French?" Max asked.

"Still fine."

"I hope I didn't wake you?"

A gravelly laugh filled the line. "Funny. I trust you found everything to your liking?"

Max smiled and I raised an eyebrow. It occurred to me that I really had no idea what Max had been up to in there.

I knew it involved Sara, but now I was beginning to wonder if the details were a bit more . . . sordid than I'd originally thought.

"It was brilliant. Bloody brilliant. As usual, of course. You have one hell of a place there."

"Good, glad to hear it. Now get to the point."

"I'd like to call in a favor."

"I assumed as much," Johnny said flatly.

"The thing is that we've found ourselves in a bit of a predicament here, and need a little help getting out of it."

"I'm listening."

"We need a distraction. A decoy."

"A distraction."

"Yes. Sara is here, as you know. But so are our friends."

"I see . . . And you'd like to ditch them."

"Not exactly. We just want them . . . entertained. One friend in particular. We'd like him safe but maybe . . . occupied for a few hours."

"So you can run off and be with your girls on Valentine's Day."

Max smiled. "Something like that."

Silence filled the line and Max and I looked up at each other in question.

"Did he hang up?" I mouthed.

Max shrugged. "Still there, mate?" he asked.

"I'm here. And yeah, no problem. Pretty sure I have the perfect distraction in mind."

"I don't trust him," I said on our way back to the restaurant.

"Stop worrying. Johnny is a man of his word, I assure you."

"He didn't exactly sound happy with you."

Max waved me off. "He's never going to be the guy to give me flowers and tell me I'm lovely."

"He sounded like we were assholes."

"We *are* arseholes."

He had a point. "So what about Henry?" I asked, stopping at the stairs just outside the restaurant.

"Do you think he'll be a problem?"

"I think if I shoved a thousand bucks in his pocket I wouldn't see him again until Tuesday morning."

"Brilliant. So we have a nice dinner, wait for Johnny to send someone over, and then find our girls. If all goes well I won't see your ugly mug until the morning, when we can start this weekend properly."

"Done." We shook hands and made our way inside with a new sense of purpose.

Will and Henry were just where I'd left them and now surrounded by a mountain of bowls and platters. There were steaks and fish, salad with bacon, steaming dishes of vegetables and what had to be some of the biggest shellfish I'd ever seen.

"Wow," Max said, looking over what had to be enough food to feed at least ten people. "Hungry?"

"We didn't know what you'd want," Henry said with a shrug. "Plus Ben's picking up the bill so . . ."

"Feeling better?" Will asked Max skeptically.

"Much, thank you. And absolutely famished."

We each took a seat and Max motioned to the waiter. "I'll have another Macallan," he said.

"And a Belvedere gimlet for me." I pointed to Henry and Will across from me. "And bring them *two* of whatever they're having."

"So what did I miss?" Max asked, covering his plate in some sort of potatoes. "Did you two finally stop playing hard to get and decide to run off together? There's a chapel just downstairs, I believe. In the casino."

"Ha," Will said. "We were actually discussing who would be next. I assured Henry here that the *only* possible answer was you."

"Oh I don't know about that," Max said. "Never know what will happen with one of your *sheduled* booty calls."

Will laughed.

"What about that, Stella? Think it'll happen with you and Sara?" Henry asked.

Max smiled but it was the shielded smile that he wore whenever he spoke about Sara. "I haven't had this conversation with her yet, I'm certainly not having it with you lot."

"But you've considered it," I found myself saying. I'd never seen Max fall for anyone like he had with Sara. I knew the feeling. He had to have at least considered it.

"Of course," he answered. "But we've only been together for a short while. We've got time."

Another round of drinks arrived and Max reached for his, holding it up for a toast. "To Bennett and Chloe. May your fights be rare, and if they aren't—because who am I kidding—at least may they be followed by some wicked shagging."

We all clinked glasses and drank deeply. The room seemed to expand and shrink, and I put my vodka down, reaching instead for my water.

"Well, I can't wait to hit the tables," Henry said, rubbing his palms together. "I spoke with a few of the dealers earlier. Kind of disappointed they have standard odds and no fire bet but hey, can't win them all."

"Wow. You sound like you've . . . really looked into this," I said, wondering for a moment if I should be legitimately concerned.

He shrugged and cut into his steak. I made a mental promise that if he started talking about card counting or needing a spotter, I'd intervene. Who said I wasn't a good brother?

We continued with dinner, Max and I sharing conspiratorial glances toward the door and back to each other. Just as Will excused himself to the restroom Max got a text.

"She's here," Max whispered. He typed something into his phone and pressed SEND. "Told Johnny what Will's wearing and that he'll be near the front of the restaurant. Showtime."

"This is too easy," I said, looking around, the tickle of uneasiness settling into my stomach. "Since meeting Chloe, nothing in my life is *ever* this easy."

"Would you relax?" he said under his breath. "This isn't insider trading, it's finding a way for us to sneak off for a shag. Calm the fuck down."

"Whoa."

I looked up at the sound of Henry's voice and followed his gaze across the room. A woman had stopped Will on his way back to the table. She was . . . *beautiful*, with miles of wavy red hair and makeup so skillfully applied she looked like a piece of art. She wore a short beaded dress that clung to her body and she smiled as she gazed at Will, her hand resting on his forearm.

But . . .

I nudged Max and pointed, sitting back when he looked up. "Is that the woman Johnny sent?"

His eyes widened before they narrowed slightly, as if he were trying to get a closer look, figure out what didn't quite add up.

"What the. . . ?" Henry said. Max began typing furiously on his phone while Henry and I continued to watch Will. The escort stood about eye level with him and had steered him toward the bar. It looked like Will might be buying her a drink. "I'm confused. Is that—?"

Will looked over at the table, meeting my eyes. And, oh, shit. In a rush I burst out laughing, understanding dawning. Johnny had totally fucked with us, and from the second the woman found him, Will knew exactly what we'd done. The gauntlet had most definitely been thrown.

"That son of a bitch," Max swore. But I didn't have time to ask because it looked like Red was ready to put the moves on Will.

We all watched in rapt silence as the escort leaned in, whispering something in his ear. Her hand was big—bigger than my own—and she placed it against his chest, fingers twisting in the fabric. Will laughed, shaking his head before nodding to us at the table.

With a seductive grin, she gripped his shirt and pulled him forward, kissing him hard on the lips. *Damn.*

He stepped away in a daze and made his way back to the table. As he took his seat we each looked at the other, unsure of what had actually happened. Will was silent for a moment, blinking several times before reaching for his drink. He drained it in one pull and then took a deep breath.

"You're a bunch of assholes," he said, leaning back in his chair and popping a shrimp into his mouth. "But as far as kissing a dude went, that actually wasn't bad."

Honestly, that one really had ended up in the Win column for Will. I glanced across the table to where he perused the dessert tray, still wearing the same smug fucking grin.

"Am I really *really* drunk or did we accidentally hire a male prostitute to distract our friend?" I asked Max.

He didn't answer, just held up his phone displaying his most recently delivered text message: a picture of Johnny's hand, middle finger extended. Perfect.

I laughed, putting my drink down with a bit more of a crash than I'd intended. "I'm not going to say I told you so but for the record, I definitely did."

"Fuck you." Max slumped back in his seat, pushing his hands into his hair. "This isn't over. He's going to bide his time, and then completely ruin us. Do you have any idea what I've done tonight to be with this woman? I snuck out on my best friend's stag weekend. I stole a limousine. I hired my other best friend a drag queen, Bennett."

Maybe it was the alcohol buzzing in my system, or the absolute absurdity of the situation, but I started to laugh, and then I couldn't stop.

"I think Ben's finally lost it," Henry said. "Who called today?" He pulled a wrinkled slip of paper from his pocket, presumably with the bets they'd each taken earlier in the day. "Damnit. It was Max."

I sat back in my seat and scrubbed my face. Max was right: this definitely wasn't over.

Six

Max Stella

The din of voices in the bar, glasses clinking, and sounds of ringing slot machines all around us was occasionally disrupted by the loud bursts of laughter by the world's biggest wanker, Will.

"Wonder what it'd be like to get head from a male prostitute?" he mused. "Like, okay, assuming of course it wasn't illegal, and you didn't even know it was a guy. I bet that would be some good suction."

I shrugged, feeling the humor of the situation bubble up inside me and burst out. "I bet it would be bloody *fantastic.*"

"Strong grip," Bennett agreed, laughing.

"Bigger tongue for the equipment if you know what I'm saying," I added.

"Well, fuck. Now you're making me wish I'd given him a go." Will picked up his empty drink glass and raised it for the waiter to bring another. "Where are we headed next?"

"Thought we could hit Tao, at the Venetian," I suggested. "Or head back to the Bellagio?"

"Does anyone actually know where Henry is?" Bennett asked, looking around for only a few seconds before seeming to decide he didn't care enough to get up.

But then Chloe and Sara appeared around a corner, arms linked and making a beeline for a blackjack table only about ten yards from the bar. Bennett straightened instinctively, drawing Will's attention.

"You've got to be fucking kidding me," Will groaned, following Ben's gaze. With mumbled thanks, he took his drink from the waiter. "They don't even know you're here, do they? Oh my God, they do. That's why you've both been idiots all night. It's like the four of you have subconscious homing devices implanted in your genitalia." He sighed. "It all makes sense now."

I stood at the same time as Bennett, stretching my arms over my head before tucking my dress shirt back into the waist of my trousers. Will could give me all the shit he wanted. I was going to Sara.

"If you don't mind, gentlemen, it looks like I'll be trying my hand at blackjack this evening."

I made my way out of the bar and to the table where the girls were organizing their chips and being dealt in. Finding a seat next to Chloe, I met Sara's eyes just a couple of seats down, giving her a little wink.

"Max," she said, simply, smiling.

"Petal," I acknowledged with a nod.

Pulling a few chips from my pocket, I had the croupier break them into smaller denominations and add me to the hand.

"I'm gonna win some money," Chloe informed the table.

"I'd love to see that," I murmured, frowning as the dealer laid down my faceup card. A five of hearts.

"As would I." Bennett slid easily into the last empty chair at the table, on the opposite side of the half circle from Chloe and beside Sara. Between me and Sara was a skinny man wearing a ten-gallon hat and one of the most fantastic bits of facial hair I'd ever seen.

When I busted with a score of twenty-five, I turned to look at the man more closely. "Mate, that is a bloody *brilliant* mustache."

He tipped his hat, thanking me before busting with a twenty-two.

Chloe held, and the dealer revealed that Chloe had both the ace and jack of spades. The house had a jack on the up card, but flipped the hole card: a king. The dealer paid out Chloe's winnings before collecting the cards on the table with a sweep of her hands.

"Told you!" Chloe sang, dancing in her seat and blowing Bennett a kiss. "It's my lucky night."

He responded with a tiny lift of his brow.

Looking across the room to the bar, I found Will,

who was sipping his drink and fucking around on his phone. He looked up and caught my eye after a moment, giving me a silent fuck-you face, and I waved, indicating that I'd be back soon.

The problem was, blackjack was fucking *fun*. Chloe was cleaning up, winning hand after hand. And although Bennett and I were systematically losing all of our money, it didn't bloody matter. The dealer was easygoing, Sara's laugh was infectious, and Mustache had started cracking the best awful jokes between each hand.

"Doctor walks into a room," he said, running his fingers over his mustache and winking at Chloe. "Says hi to the patient on the exam table, goes to make note of something on his chart."

The dealer dealt our facedown cards and we all looked at the table in time to see the next cards arriving faceup.

"He realizes he's holding a thermometer and frowns. 'Well, fuck,' he says, 'some asshole's got my pen.'"

And because her sense of humor was always easy and gutter-loving, Sara completely lost it, falling onto the soft padded edge of the table in laughter and looking lovelier than I think she had all night. She was flushed from whatever she'd had to drink, but even more than that, she looked positively blissful. When she looked up and caught me staring, her smile straightened as if liquid heat had trickled into her veins, and she blinked down to look at my mouth. Going back to find her at the theater had been the best decision of my night.

Come to think of it, the only good one. I gave her a wink, licked my lips.

"You two going to fornicate or play some goddamn cards?" Chloe asked, having decided to stay with a nine showing; the table showed a six, and busted, hitting seven on top of a hole card of nine.

"Shut your gob, woman," I hissed playfully.

"A young guy walks into a bar," our new acquaintance started as the dealer cleared the hand, and *fuck* I'd decided this was the best man ever to have at a blackjack table. The dealer began the process of shuffling the decks. "He orders ten shots of whiskey. The bartender says, 'Damn, kid,' but lines them up anyway."

I liked Mustache because of said mustache of course, but also the fact that he looked like he spent a lot of birthdays alone. He had a way about him that mixed ease and desperation, and yet here he was, cracking dirty jokes with perfect finesse with a bunch of half-sloshed strangers. I didn't even mind his gaze turning dopey and loaded when he turned and smiled at Sara. Couldn't blame the bloke; I had no choice but to fall for her; Sara was as irresistible as gravity.

"So here they are: ten shots in front of this skinny beanpole kid. The kid knocks them all back one after the other, barely blinking. 'Wow,' says the barman, 'what're you celebrating?'"

Sara was already laughing, and I turned to watch her in wonder. She would never stop being a tangle of mystery, this one, anticipating dirty jokes told by an eccentric stranger in Vegas.

Mustache chuckled, shaking his head. "'My first blow job,' says the kid. The bartender looks surprised and says, 'In that case let me buy you another.'" He stopped looking over at Sara expectantly.

And with both hands in the air as if dancing in victory, Sara yelled, "Kid shakes his head. 'No thanks, man. If ten shots won't get rid of the taste, another won't make a lick of difference!'"

Around us, laughter roared and I realized that we had begun to attract quite a crowd to the table. Chloe was on a roll, Mustache was aces, and at nearly two in the morning, we were clearly the table having the most fun in the casino. Sara and Mustache high-fived as the dealer began flipping out the cards, wearing an amused smile.

The card play turned into a blur of jokes and drinks; Chloe whooping in celebration was interrupted often by sound of Sara's loud, hysterical laugh. With a jerk of awareness, I turned, looking for Will at the bar. It had been a long while since I indicated we'd be done soon, and I'd completely lost track of time.

He was gone.

I pulled my phone out of my pocket, glancing up with resignation at my two remaining twenty-five-dollar chips, and texted him, We're set. Where are you?

He texted back a few moments later, Meet you at the Venetian. I'm getting head from a dude.

"Arsehole," I mumbled, just as Mustache started a new joke.

But the sound of his voice beside me fell silent as a hand wrapped around my shoulder. "Mr. Stella."

The table and the boisterous crowd went silent. I caught a look of concern on Sara's face just as I looked up, turning to see a man wearing a dark tailored suit and a very serious expression.

"Yeah, mate?"

He wore an earpiece and an expression that communicated I was meant to take him very bloody seriously. "I'm going to have to ask you and Mr. Ryan to come with me, please."

"What's this about?" Bennett asked, laying his cards face down on the table. The crowd broke out into speculating whispers.

"I'm not at liberty to discuss it out here on the floor. I'll ask you once again, gentlemen, to follow me. Now."

Without further question, we stood, exchanging baffled looks and following the man away from the table. I turned, giving Sara an encouraging smile, mouthing, "It's fine."

What, after all, could we possibly have done?

The man in the black suit led us through a service doorway, down a long, empty corridor, and then through an unlabeled door. Inside the stark, white room was a metal table not unlike the one I'd started my evening with, and three metal folding chairs.

"Have a seat." The man indicated that we each sit in one of the chairs, and then turned to leave.

"What's going on?" Bennett asked. "We've followed you here readily out of courtesy. The least you can do is tell us why you asked us to leave the table."

"Wait for Hammer." The man nodded toward the remaining empty chair, and then left.

I settled back into my seat while Bennett stood, pacing for a few quiet minutes before sighing, and sitting down next to me again. He pulled his phone from his pocket and texted something, presumably to Chloe.

"This is a load of shit," he grumbled.

I made a noise of agreement, but then stopped from saying more when we heard footsteps coming down the hall toward us.

Two guys walked through the door, both sporting dark suits, short-cropped hair, and hands the size of watermelons. Neither man was taller than me, but I had the distinct impression they had more hand-to-hand combat training than did I. Which is to say, some.

They stared at us for what seemed like full, heavy minutes of silence. Assessing. I felt sweat bead at my forehead, wondering if these men were the owners of the limo I'd . . . *borrowed* for my short romp with Sara. They were definitely either limo drivers or hit men.

Or, perhaps, they were undercover policemen here to reprimand us for hiring a prostitute. Had we actually paid for her? Could she be traced to us? Or . . . bollocks. Maybe Sara and I had been caught on camera and they were here to bust us for our public escapades earlier. I mentally filed through the phone calls I would need to make once booked on charges of public indecency. Lawyer, Sara, Mum, smug business partner, hysterical sisters. And then I saw the image of all the creepy mug shots in the paper of men and women arrested for fucking in cars, or on bridges, or on school grounds and realized *this* is why Sara and I kept our activities to Johnny's club. There, we'd never see a man in a suit coming to reprimand us; Johnny would shut that nonsense down before the police even had time to enter the club's coordinates into their GPS.

I glanced at Bennett, who, now that the men had

joined the room, was sitting in his own chair looking as relaxed as he would be at the head of a boardroom table. He had one hand in his pocket, the other resting on his thigh, and was staring evenly up at the two men in front of us.

"Good evening, gentlemen," I said, deciding someone needed to start the festivities. The guys were hulks, brutes, goons, getting their ideas for facial expressions from comic books or Tarantino films. It was almost too easy to want to have fun, just a little.

The first one to speak was the shorter of the two—though by no means *short*—and had a voice about as deep as a five-year-old girl's. "I'm Hammer. This here is Kim."

Beside me, Bennett Ryan was just drunk enough to say, "I appreciate the irony of that. On both counts."

The man who introduced himself as Hammer stared at Bennett for a long pause before asking, "Any idea why we asked Leroy to bring the two of you back here?"

I answered, "Uh, no?" just as Bennett answered, "Well, it's definitely not because we cleaned out the house."

When he said that, and for the first time since we were brought back into the room, it occurred to me that we were more likely here for gambling-associated reasons than grand theft auto or public indecency. Instead of being booked and ultimately released, we were going to have our fingers broken one by one by a eunuch named Hammer and a brute named Kim. Brilliant.

Hammer smirked, saying, "Do you have any idea how many assholes like you we see back here? Out for a weekend with their STD-infested douche-bag friends, thinking they'll use their brand-new copy of *Card Counting for Dummies* to clean out the house so they can go back and bang their ugly-ass girlfriends and impress them with the five hundred dollars they won?"

Clearing his throat with authority, Bennett asked, "Do we really look to you like two men who would find thrill in winning five hundred dollars?"

Kim, who was somehow both much larger and less intimidating than Hammer because of the rubies in both of his ears, lurched forward, slamming his fists down on the table, making the entire fucking *room* shake. I couldn't help but notice that Bennett barely flinched at all. I sure as hell jumped; I'd been convinced the metal table was going to collapse on our legs.

"You think this is your motherfucking mommy's house?" Kim growled, his voice as low and gravelly as Hammer's was girlish. "You think you're playing Go Fish at a fucking linoleum table?"

Bennett sat motionless, his face impassive.

The man turned to me, eyebrows raised as if I was meant to speak for both of us.

"No," I said, giving my best, relaxed smile. "If we were at my mum's house we would have been offered chips and Guinness."

Ignoring my wisecrack, Hammer stepped forward. "What do you think the house does when we get card counters in here?"

"Mate, I wouldn't know how to count cards even if I was trained by fucking Rain Man. The repercussions are beyond me."

"You think you're funny?"

I sat back in my chair, exhaling heavily. This was pants. "I think I'm *baffled*. I lost all my chips. Even if we were counting cards, we're not exactly good at it, so I can't quite suss out what we're doing here."

"The best counters let themselves lose sometimes. You think by counting you'll only ever win?"

I sighed, leaning forward, my elbows resting on my knees. This was going nowhere with the continued rhetorical questions. "Can I tell you a secret?"

Hammer looked surprised, straightening. "Go."

"I've never played blackjack in my life before tonight. This one?" I said, nodding to Bennett. "He negotiates drink prices when we're sitting at a table and they're *already free*. He doesn't fucking *gamble*."

Snorting, Kim said, "And yet here you are, in a two-deck pitch, you stand on s-seventeen, double after split."

Bennett leaned forward, genuinely curious. "Was that English?"

For the first time since we walked in here, I saw the corner of Kim's lips twitch as if repressing a smile. Or a snarl. I couldn't actually be sure.

"I'm going to give you two choices," Hammer said. "One, I break your fingers. Or two, I break your face."

I blinked, feeling a brief moment of pride that I had correctly predicted our punishment. But something felt *off.* Just because I hadn't played blackjack in Vegas before didn't mean I had been living under a rock. Finger-and face-breaking seemed a touch off-protocol for a couple of guys suspected of counting cards.

"Let's see your hands," Kim said, patting the table.

"You're delusional," Bennett replied, laughing incredulously.

"I'll start with the pinkie," Hammer said, lips twitching. "No one needs their pinkie."

"Get stuffed, all right?" I growled, feeling a disorienting mix of impatience and righteous indignation building in my chest. "Forget the accent, I'm a fucking American citizen, you arseholes—I know my rights. If you're going to start talking about getting violent, get a fucking cop or lawyer in here."

The door swung open, and bloody *Will* entered,

clapping slowly. Ice trickled into my veins, and I leaned back in my chair with a harsh exhale.

"Oh, you wanker," I sighed.

"It was perfect!" He smiled at Hammer and Kim, and I groaned, dropping my head onto my arms on the table. I should have known. "You were angry, but convincing," he said to me. "You might have thrown in an indignant fist slam for full effect, but I really like what you did with the American-citizen bit. Really got me right here." I looked up just as he tapped his chest, over his heart, eyes soft and praising.

While Hammer and Kim stepped to the side, laughing, Bennett stood, walking over to Will. For a second I wondered if he was going to punch him or maybe just kick Will in the goolies, but then I realized he was smiling. He looked Will in the eye for a count of about three, and then patted his shoulder before simply walking to the door. "Well played," he murmured before disappearing down the hall.

Hammer and Kim moved to me, hands extended and smiles full and easy now. "Sorry, man," Hammer said, laughing. "Mr. Johnny French called. Said we needed to help your friend Will even the score. Apparently you deserved some payback for acting like pussy-whipped little babies earlier?" He held his hands up, shrugging in a way that made me wonder whether he was officially associated with the mob. "We just wanted to fuck with you a little."

"Seemed the easiest way to get you away from the ladies," Will said, rocking on his heels.

I sighed, rubbing my face and feeling my heart rate slowly return to normal. All said, this was a pretty brilliant prank. "Well, while you had us back here, I'm pretty sure Chloe was out there cleaning up."

"She did pretty well," Will agreed. "Few thousand at least."

"Come on," Kim said, helping me up and slapping my back. "Go out there and get drunk."

"I'll tell you what," I said, returning his handshake. "I'm staying the fuck away from cards."

"I'm an American citizen!" Will yelled, and then collapsed into the couch in hysterics. It was probably the tenth time he'd made this proclamation in the past fifteen minutes.

"So," I began. "You paid those men a hundred dollars to scare the piss out of us. How'd that work out for you?"

Ignoring me, Will pretended to wipe away a tear. "Your patriotic battle cry at the end is going to stay with me for all my days."

"It was pretty amazing," Bennett agreed.

We sat around a low glass table in a posh bar at the Bellagio, lounging on soft suede couches and sipping what felt like our millionth cocktail of the night. My inebriation snuck up on me; until this moment, I hadn't really felt it. But with my adrenaline slowly slipping from my veins, and knowing the girls were safely somewhere in their beds, my limbs grew heavy with the effects of our adventures, and the accumulated alcohol.

All around us, the bar was quiet; it was well past three in the morning, and most of the people remaining were in the casino, or at one of the more wild bars.

From the corner of my eye, I saw a man approach our table. He wore a tailored suit, an earpiece, and had the distinct look of importance about him; the waiters made room for him, all offered him nervous hellos. Clearly someone of circumstance was headed our way, and since Will was seated at the table with us, I was disinclined to think he was fucking with us again.

"Gentlemen," the man said, standing at the head of the table. "You must be Bennett, Max, and Will."

We all nodded, sharing pleasantries.

"The elder Mr. Ryan has joined us in the high rollers room," he then said. So that's where Henry had gotten to. "But his phone is dead, and he asked me to come check on you. My name is Michael Hawk, and I'm the vice president of client relations here at the Bellagio."

I chanced a look at my friends, to see when they

registered that, with some people in his life, this man might be known as Mike Hawk. Will closed his eyes for a beat, swallowed with effort, and then opened them again, containing himself. Bennett nodded, and to my complete fascination, had to bite his top lip to repress any further reaction.

"I wanted to make sure that you were enjoying your night," Mr. Hawk continued, looking at each of us in turn.

"It's been fantastic," I answered, unable to look away from Bennett. I hadn't seen anything like this from him in at least a decade: his lip shook, he covered it with his finger, and his eyes started to water. Finally, he looked over to me . . . and then he absolutely fucking *broke.*

With a hand splayed over his face, Ben leaned back into the sofa and shook with laughter, just drunk enough, and tired enough, and full up to fucking *here* with the insanity of the night to completely lose his shit over some guy named Mike Hawk standing in front of us. Beside him, Will turned red before bending and covering his face with both hands.

"I'm sorry," Will gasped from behind his fingers. "I don't mean to be rude, Mr. Hawk. It's just too much."

Turning back up to the man beside our table, I smiled. "Thanks very much for checking in. Go ahead and let Henry know we're sorted."

Mike Hawk wasn't a tall man, and he didn't look as hard and intimidating as the casino executives in movies would lead me to expect. He was average height, with a round, friendly face and eyes full of understanding. He gave a little laugh, shaking his head before leaving us with, "Enjoy your stay, gentlemen."

"I would like to state for the record," I started once he'd left, "that I am the only fucking bloke at this table who was able to keep his arse together."

"Mike Hawk!" Bennett practically yelled at me, dropping his hand. His eyes were red from laughing. "How am I supposed to keep it together over that? That's like meeting a fucking ***unicorn***."

Will leaned over to high-five him, and then sighed, leaning his head back against the back of the couch. "Holy crap that may have been the highlight of the night."

"The night is young," Bennett said, recovering with only a slight slur to his words. He glanced at Will's empty glass. "Have another."

"No. It's too late to get me drunk and have your wicked way with me."

"Garçon!" I yelled, grinning. "A scotch for the curmudgeon. Bring the whole bottle if you would."

"I told you, Max, I'm not drinking that." Will turned his face away in mock anger. "It's too damn late to pretend you love me."

The waiter slid the glass of scotch in front of Will and, with a quiet clink, set the entire bottle beside it.

Will stared at me, at the bottle, and then shook his head. "No."

"The thing is," Will slurred, tossing a sloppy arm around my shoulders. "Women are *tricky*." He waved the index finger of his free hand in front of my face. "How often do you meet one you can imagine just hanging out with like *this*?" He dragged the *s* out to about five seconds, and then lurched forward, reaching for his glass. It skittered away from his fingertips before he finally captured it with his palm.

"Just the one," I admitted. "And even with Sara, it's different than with you guys. I try to curb the swearing." I rubbed my jaw, reconsidering. "Sort of."

"You curbing the swearing is like me curbing the . . ." Will trailed off, thinking. "The something. I'm hungry." He ran a hand over his face and looked at his watch. Likewise, I checked my phone. It was nearly five thirty in the morning. "Actually, I'm tired. Let's meet for lunch at noon and start this fucking bachelor party thing over again tomorrow."

The three of us stood, closed out our tab, and made our way toward the bank of elevators, each of us scrambling in our pockets to find our room key to show security.

We stood in silence as the doors opened. I was blissfully tipsy and ready for a good snog with my lady upstairs. I almost couldn't wait to see what we could stir up tomorrow.

Seven

Bennett Ryan

Will's voice broke the silence in the elevator. "Should we be even mildly concerned about Henry down there in the high rollers room?"

I reached into my jacket pocket, pulling out my brother's credit card—the only one Mina let him leave home with. "I have no idea what he's playing, but he'll either keep winning or run out of money and the only card he'll have in his wallet will be the one that opens his hotel room door."

"Brilliant," Max murmured, sleepily leaning into the wall of the elevator car. "I'm fucking knackered."

Will sighed, watching the numbers climb on the digital display. "You know, for being a couple of neutered assholes, you guys actually managed to make a pretty entertaining night out of it."

"Nudie club, fake medical emergencies, fan-fucking-tastic dinner, grand theft auto, transvestite escort, Chloe wins a few grand, and we nearly get maimed by some goons," Max said, standing up straighter. "Not so bad, eh?"

Will turned to stare at him. "Grand theft auto?"

Max rubbed his face, shaking his head. "A story for another—"

Will held up a hand, eyes wide as if he'd already moved on from his first question. "And how could you forget Mike Hawk? I think, especially for the two of you, *Mike Hawk* figured quite prominently in this evening's activities." Will hiccupped, weaving slightly as the doors to our floor opened. "I'd say you're pussy-whipped, but I think it's even worse than that."

I watched as Max's smile went from self-satisfied to mocking. "Will. *Darling*." He put a heavy hand on Will's cheek and clucked his tongue. "I can't wait for that one girl to come in and kick your feet out from under you. You think you have things organized, sorted. You think you're content with your low-key bachelor apartment, with your triathlons and your work and your scheduled pussy. When *that one girl* comes along, I'm going to say I told you so, and give you no bloody sympathy when you've turned into a lovesick strop." With a light slap to Will's cheek, he stepped away, laughing as he walked down the hall. "Can't fucking *wait* for it, mate."

Will watched Max's heavy limbs and dragging feet, and then turned to me expectantly as if I would add to the lecture. I shrugged. "Pretty much what he said. When you find that girl, we'll be happy for you, but mostly we'll be happy to give you endless shit."

"This is why you're my people," he mumbled, punching

me weakly in the chest before turning the opposite way down the hall.

Bidding Will good night, I walked to my room, wishing I knew where Chloe was staying. Even as exhausted and half drunk as I was, I still would have gone downstairs and climbed in a cab to go anywhere to her.

Just inside my door, I stopped at my closet to hang up my blazer, and froze. Dangling from a wooden hanger was Chloe's lingerie from the club, the jewel stones of the tiny bra and underwear winking green and white in the dim light coming in the bedroom window.

I moved farther into the room, wanting to confirm what my racing pulse had concluded: she was here, in my bed, waiting for me. Sure enough, a Chloe-shaped lump was sound asleep amid a mountain of blankets and pillows in the middle of the king mattress.

Stripping my clothes off and leaving them in a discarded pile on the floor, I climbed over her, braced on my arms and legs. Not touching her, not yet, just taking her in: a tangle of brown curls against the stark white bed linens, eyes closed but lids fluttering in her dreams, lips wet and red and begging to be kissed. Everything below her neck was covered by her cocoon of blankets, and when I stared down at the steady rhythm of her pulse beneath the delicate skin of her neck, I felt a little predatory. The thrill of being able to do this—kiss her, wake her up, fuck her—was still as fresh tonight as it was nearly two years ago when, for the first time, we finally had time alone in a hotel.

Lifting the covers, I slid in beside her and realized she was wearing nothing but my shirt. Beneath, her body was bare. It was one of my favorite iterations of Chloe: when her limbs were heavy and slow from sleep, her sounds similarly deeper, more wanton.

I inched down beneath the covers only as she began to be aware that I was in bed with her. She'd bathed; she no longer smelled of an unfamiliar woman but of her own soap now, blossom and citrus. I kissed the curve of her breast over the shirt, lifted the cotton to lick a line from her belly button to the sweetness of her hip.

Curious fingers ran through my hair; fingertips grazed along my jaw and moved up to trace the shape of my mouth. "I thought I was dreaming," she whispered, rising into consciousness.

"Not dreaming."

Her hands found my hair, her legs opened wide beneath the covers because she knew now that I was there, and that I was going to give her what she loved more than almost anything on the planet. Shifting so I was lying between her legs, I bent and blew a soft stream of air across her pussy, teasing and relishing how she bowed off the bed for me, urging me closer, offering her little broken sounds of pleasure. It was a dance I loved: kissing her hips, her thighs, exhaling oh-so-close to that sweet, tiny slide of skin. The room was cool but her skin was already damp with perspiration, and with a single finger I easily slid through the heat of her sex. My Chloe cried out, in a tangle of relief and need.

She didn't urge me faster because if she'd learned anything, it's that I would just slow down. She was in my bed, in my room, already my wife for all intents and purposes, and no way was I rushing this when I'd been thinking of her all night, and had nowhere to be early tomorrow morning—*this* morning—except in bed with her.

I let her feel my breath and my fingers, kissed her stomach, tasted her skin. *Fuck, she's beautiful,* I thought, with her arms stretched over her head, her hands searching for the anchor the rest of her didn't seem to feel. Her hips rolled in front of me, searching, and finally I couldn't take the seduction of her, the warmth and sweetness anymore. I kissed her gently just once, closing my eyes against the intensity of it.

I wanted more. I wanted, as always, to find a way to taste and fuck her simultaneously and the second my tongue slipped out to glide across the small rise of her clit I was fucking done, mouth open and sucking, devouring. With a cry, she dug her hands fully into my hair, hips sliding and rocking into me and it became a rhythm we fell into without effort, without stutter. She was silky and warm and her legs found their way over my shoulders, down my back, closing around me until the only thing I could hear was the muffled sound of her pleas, the rustle of sheets beneath her as she moved up into me.

Her body couldn't decide what it wanted—tongue or the pressure of my lips—so I made the decision for her, hungry after a night of secretive, hurried sex and so little intimacy. I surrounded her with my mouth, sucking and reminding her *this is how I love you, both soft and wild.*

I am fucking lost in you.

Her body was so familiar to me, its dips and curves, the flavor of her sex as she went from sleeping to wild. And although I'd started this wanting to tease her, I couldn't; her release was a precursor to mine. She came quickly, legs falling away, back bowed until her cries quieted and thighs stopped trembling. She propped herself up on her elbows, watching me.

I kissed up her navel, pushing my shirt up her body as I went, and exposing the soft fullness of her breasts.

"Hello, my lovelies."

"Did you have fun tonight?" she asked, voice still groggy with sleep and pleasure.

"It was definitely interesting." My teeth found the bottom swell of her breast, and then my tongue slid up the curve, found her nipple.

"Bennett?"

I paused my gentle attack on her chest to look up and catch the uncertainty on her face. "Hmm?"

"Is it really okay that we did this? That I crashed your

bachelor party? I mean, it basically hijacked your first night here."

"Do you think I'm at all surprised you decided to take charge at the club?"

She closed her eyes, smiling a little. But only a little. "Not being surprised isn't the same thing as being glad that I did it."

I pushed my shirt the rest of the way up her arms, trapping her wrists above her head and using it to tie her hands together. "We have all weekend to celebrate the bachelor thing. It's really okay that you did this." I leaned down, sucked her neck. "In fact, if you ever stop doing crazy things like that, stop being wild and foolish because you want me so much, it might just ruin me a little."

"A little?" I could hear the smile in her voice.

Looking down at her face, at her hair fanned across the pillow, eyes heavy with desire and satisfaction in equal measure, I had the sense of being pulled backward through a cable in time. How the fuck had we gotten here? This woman beneath me was the same one I'd despised so viciously for months, the one I'd fucked with such combustible need and hate. And now, she was in my room, on the weekend of my bachelor party, wearing my grandmother's ring, hands tied over her head with my favorite T-shirt, the one she'd claimed as her own months ago.

Chloe tilted her head, catching my eye. "Where did you go?"

I closed my eyes, swallowing. "Just remembering."

She waited, eyes studying me.

"I was just remembering everything and . . ."

"And?"

"Thinking about how we started . . . and what it was like before. I was trying to remember the last woman I was with before you. . . . I don't think I ever told you about that night."

Beneath me, she laughed. "This has the potential to be *such* a romantic conversation." She wiggled a little, rubbing her slick skin along the underside of my cock.

"Just listen," I murmured, bending to kiss her. Pulling back, I said, "She was my date at the fund-raiser for Millennium Organics. You were there, too. . . ."

"I remember," she whispered, watching my lips.

"You had on this dress . . ." I exhaled. "*Fuck*. That dress. It was—"

"Red."

"Yes. But not just red. Fire engine red. *Siren* red. You looked like a fucking beacon, a devil . . . which is pretty appropriate, considering. Anyway, Amber was my date, and—"

"Blond. Tall. Fake boobs?" she asked, clearly remembering. I took a small bit of pleasure knowing she was paying close enough attention even then to remember my date nearly two years later.

"That's her. And she was . . ." I sighed, remembering my complete apathy that entire evening. "She was nice enough. But she wasn't *you*. I was obsessed with you, but in a *really* fucked-up way. I loved finding ways to push your buttons just to see you react to me for a second. I loved getting a rise out of you, because I think it meant that I was the focus of your thoughts for a moment, however rage-filled."

She laughed again, stretching to kiss my neck, sucking lightly. "Psychopath."

"That night," I continued, ignoring her, "you were getting a drink at the bar, and I walked up to you and made some crack—I don't even remember now what it was I'd said. But I'm sure it was nasty, and unnecessary." I closed my eyes, remembering her face, how she stared at me blankly, without even a trace of interest. "You looked at me and then *laughed* before taking your drink and just walking away. It fucking wrecked me, I think, though I didn't really get that until later. I was used to seeing you react to my jabs with a tiny hint of hurt feelings, anger, or frustration. But to see absolutely nothing but indifference . . . fuck. That was it for me."

"I don't remember what you said, either," she admitted. "But I'm sure it took a lot of effort for me to look unaffected."

"We left not long after that. Amber and I." I smoothed a hand up Chloe's body, over her breast to her face. I looked her in the eye and admitted, "I fucked her. But it was awful. You kept barging into my head. I would close my eyes and imagine what it would be like to touch you. I tried to imagine the sounds you would make when you'd come, how you would feel. That's when *I* came. I bit the pillow to keep from saying your name."

She exhaled sharply, and I realized she'd been holding her breath. "Did you go to her place or yours?"

I looked away from where my fingers ran over her jaw and met her eyes again. How was that relevant? "Hers. Why?"

Shrugging, she whispered, "Just curious."

I continued to study her and could see the wheels turning, some private curiosity growing in her thoughts.

Bending to kiss her ear, I asked, "What are you thinking, little devil?"

She smiled up at me, caught. "I was wondering . . . what position you were in."

Ice trickled into my bloodstream. "Do you like hearing about this because you want to imagine me with another woman?"

She shook her head immediately, eyes darkening. Her hands turned into tight fists around the knot of my shirt above her head. "I like hearing how you were thinking about *me*. I just . . . want to hear about it."

"I was on top of her, like this," I murmured, wary. "We only had sex that one time. I'm sure she found me wholly unimpressive as a lover."

She wiggled, adjusting the position of her hands in their soft binding, watching me. *Thinking, thinking, thinking*. "Before you had sex with her," she said, eyes on my mouth. "When you got back to her place. Did she go down on you?"

Shrugging, I admitted, "I think so. A little."

"And did you?"

"Taste her?" I asked and Chloe nodded. "No," I said. "I didn't."

"Did you wear a condom?"

"I always wore a condom," I said, laughing. "Well, before you."

She smiled and rolled her eyes. "Right." But then her legs slid up around my waist. "Before *me*." All I needed to do was shift my hips slightly and I would be able to press inside her. Yet somehow, talking about this naked and over her felt perfect. We had no secrets. "Did she come?" she asked.

Sighing, I admitted, "She faked it."

Chloe laughed, head pressed back into the pillow so she could see me better. "You're sure?"

"Positive. It was an impressive effort if not a bit over-the-top."

"Poor girl didn't know what she was missing then."

"It was only a few days before the conference room," I whispered, kissing the corner of her mouth. "I think I was probably already in love with you. So when I think back to that night with Amber, it feels as though I cheated. Given how you found me tonight—blindfolded, passively accepting an erotic dance—I want to air all of my potential sins. I guess that's why I'm talking about Amber now."

Her face straightened, eyes wide and earnest. "Babe.

You *didn't* cheat. Either with Amber or if had been another woman tonight dancing for you."

"I wouldn't, you know," I said, my voice tight. Reaching above her, I untied her hands, rubbing her wrists carefully. "You saw that I wasn't aroused until I knew it was you. I *couldn't* be unfaithful to you."

She nodded, and I kissed up her neck to her swollen lips. Swollen from the rough treatment I gave her not long ago. *Holy shit she must be sore everywhere.* Even still, she lowered her arms, reached between us, and rubbed me over the crease of her sex.

When she kissed me, she moaned quietly against my tongue. "You taste like me."

"However could that have happened?" I asked, nibbling her bottom lip.

Angling her hips, she pushed up into me, suddenly demanding and urgent.

"Easy," I whispered, pulling back and sinking into her slowly, groaning into her neck. "Don't go too fast." *Fuck.* She even felt like honey, smooth and sweet. "So good. Always so fucking good, Chlo."

"How did you know?"

I paused for a moment as I pulled my hips back, interpreting her question. "How did I know you're sore?"

She nodded.

It was her favorite game, the one where I told her every tiny thing I noticed. I paid attention; she loved it.

"You rode my fingers pretty hard earlier."

She hummed, eyes closed and hands running down my back.

"And I wasn't particularly gentle in the restroom."

"You really weren't," she whispered, turning her head to suck on my shoulder.

I started an easy, steady rhythm moving in her. "So just now, when I put my mouth on you? I wasn't surprised you were a little swollen."

"Close. Faster, please, baby," she gasped, but I didn't pick up speed.

"Not faster," I objected, lips near her ear. "It's the slow sex that drives me most wild. It's when I can feel you best, hear every sound you're making. I can imagine how we might look beneath the blankets, where I'm moving in you. I think about how many times I'll make you come. I don't have all of those thoughts when I'm fucking you hard in a bed, or in a bathroom of a casino."

Her breath faltered, and she held it, silently begging me to get her there. She ran her hands up my back, around my neck to my face. I felt the cool press of her engagement ring, thinking *holy shit, this woman is going to be my wife, have my children, share my home and my life. She'll see me grow old and most likely insane. She'll promise to love me through all of it.*

I lifted myself above her, arms straight so I could watch

what I was feeling, moving inside her. But her hands cupped my face, brought my attention back to her eyes.

"Hey."

I tried to catch my breath, felt sweat drop from my forehead onto her chest. "Yeah?"

She licked her lips, swallowed. "I am so in love with you." Her thumb slipped into my mouth and I bit down sharply, causing her to let out a tight moan. "And whatever happens outside of this, of us like this . . ."

"I know."

We shared a desperate look, a mutual, silent agreement that we would never get enough, that maybe the ideal life was us here like this, alone and touching, but it would never be our reality to exist here exclusively. It was why she crashed my bachelor party but would leave tomorrow. It was why I couldn't stay away, knowing she was in the same city.

And here she was, limbs heavy and fevered beneath me, hips rising urgently up to mine to get what she needed. She would always belong to me—at home, at work, in bed—and that thought sent me barreling down the road to my release.

She was close, but unfortunately I was closer. "Get there, sweet thing. I . . . I can't . . ."

Her hands gripped my hips, head pushing back into the pillow. "Please."

My body tensed, hips thrusting wildly, my orgasm held back by barely a thread. "Fucking get there, Mills."

It was the voice I used sparingly because I never wanted it to lose its effect on her. With a flush down her chest, she arched off the bed, pulling her thighs high up against her body to send me deep into her. With her lips parting in a sharp cry, she dissolved into her orgasm beneath me.

I'd never tire of the view of Chloe coming. The blush on her skin, the nearly drugged darkness of her eyes as she watched me, and the way her lips shaped my name . . . Every fucking time it reminded me that I was the only man to ever give her pleasure like this. Her arms fell away, heavy with exhaustion, and her tongue peeked out to wet her lips.

"Fuck," she whispered, shaking.

Relief washed through me, opening the floodgates and permitting my own body to tumble forward, blind to everything but the sensation of her around me. The sweetness of her, the wetness of her . . . My back bowed back as I came, shouting out into the quiet, sterile room.

The sound of my yell echoed from the ceiling when I collapsed onto her, sweaty and heavy. I wanted to nestle my face into the smooth curve of her neck and sleep for at least three days.

She laughed, groaning under my weight. "Get off me, Hulk."

I rolled away, practically crashing into the mattress beside her. "Damn, Chlo. That was . . ."

She curled into me, purring, "Very, *very* good." Stretching to nibble at my jaw, she whispered, "I'm going to need at least ten minutes before we do that again."

I laughed, and then it turned into a hoarse cough as the idea hit me fully. "Jesus, woman. I may need a bit longer than that. Just fucking cuddle me for a few."

With a small kiss to my neck, she whispered, "I can't wait for you to become Mr. Bennett Mills."

My eyes flew open. "What?"

Her laugh was low and husky against my skin. "You heard me."

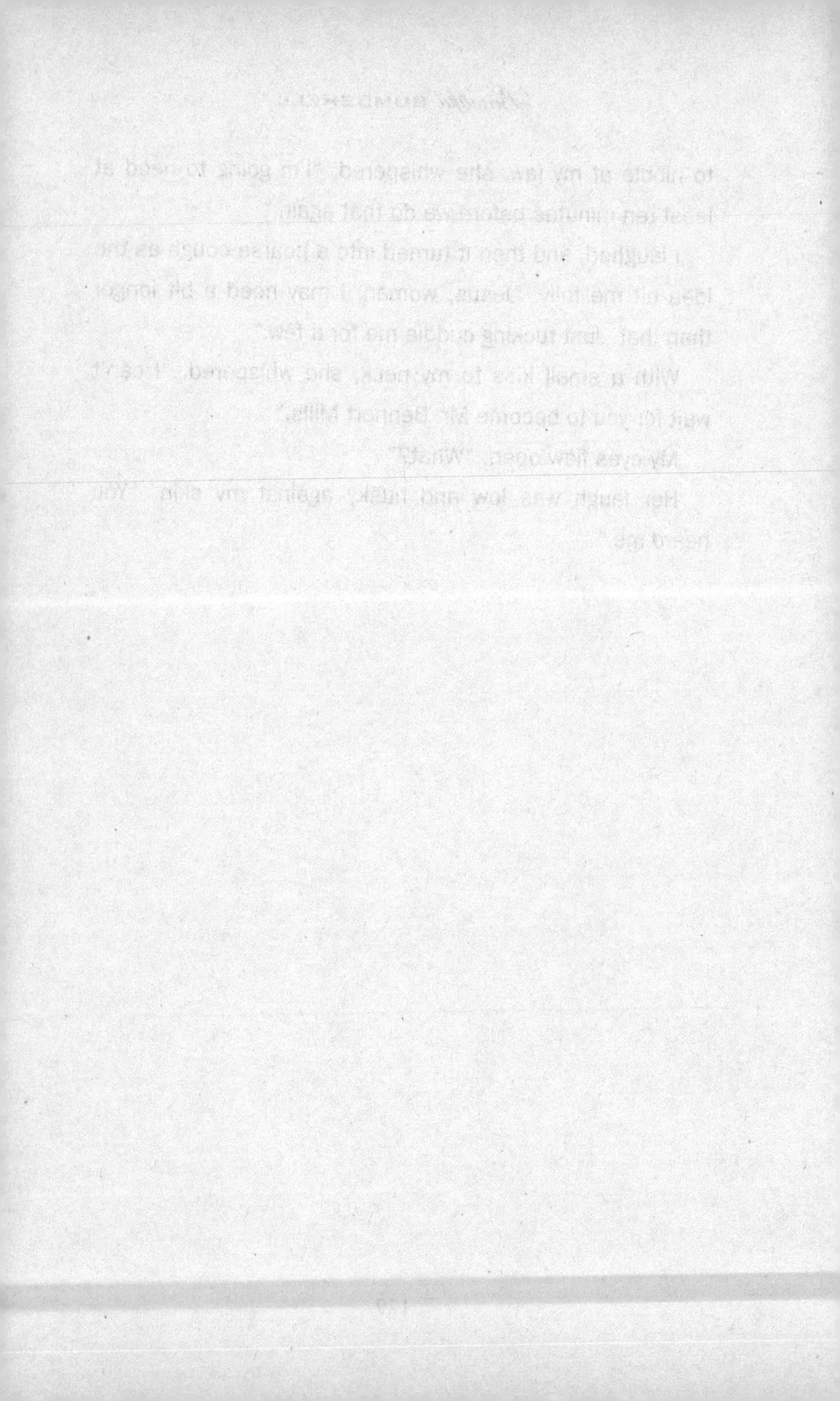

Acknowledgments

Thanks to our agent, Holly Root, to our partners in crime (husbands and kiddos), to our fantastic readers, and to our friends and family who put up with our glassy-eyed stares when we're mentally plotting another chapter during a lunch date.

Thanks to every single wonderful person at Gallery. Thank you, Jen and Lauren.

And thank you most of all to our editor, Adam Wilson, who appreciates that knickers are best in a bunch.

Hot on the heels of *Beautiful Bombshell* comes Will's story.

Will this chronic Casanova finally meet his match in a bookish bombshell?

Take a sneak peek here at the opening chapter of *Beautiful Player* . . .

THE SEQUEL TO
BEAUTIFUL BASTARD
AND BEAUTIFUL STRANGER
CHRISTINA
LAUREN
New York Times
bestselling author
"Deliciously
steamy."
–EW.com on
Beautiful Bastard
Beautiful
PLAYER

Prologue

Hanna

We were in the ugliest apartment in all of Manhattan, and it wasn't just that my brain was especially programmed away from art appreciation: objectively these paintings were *all* hideous. A hairy leg growing from a flower stem. A mouth with spaghetti pouring out. Beside me, my oldest brother and my father hummed thoughtfully, nodding as if they understood what they were seeing. I was the one who kept us moving forward; it seemed to be the unspoken protocol that party guests should make the circuit, admire the art, and only *then* feel free to enjoy the appetizers being carried on trays around the room.

But at the very end, above the massive fireplace and between two garish candelabras, was a painting of a double helix—the structure of the DNA molecule—and printed across the entire canvas was a quote by Tim Burton: *We all know interspecies romance is weird.*

Thrilled, I laughed, turning to Jensen and Dad. "Okay. *That* one is good."

Jensen sighed. "You *would* like that."

I glanced to the painting and back to my brother. "Why? Because it's the only thing in this entire place that makes any sense?"

He looked at Dad and something passed between them, some permission granted from father to son. "We need to talk to you about your relationship to your job."

It took a minute before his words, his tone, and his determined expression triggered my understanding. "Jensen," I said. "Are we really going to have this conversation *here*?"

"Yes, here." His green eyes narrowed. "It's the first time I've seen you out of the lab in the past two days when you weren't sleeping or scarfing down a meal."

I'd often noted how it seemed the most prominent personality traits of my parents—vigilance, drive, impulse, charm, and caution—had been divided cleanly and without contamination among their five offspring.

Vigilance and *Drive* were headed into battle in the middle of a Manhattan soiree.

"We're at a party, Jens. We're supposed to be talking about how wonderful the art is," I countered, waving vaguely to the walls of the opulently furnished living room. "And how scandalous the . . . something . . . is." I had no idea what the latest gossip was, and this little white flag of ignorance just proved my brother's point.

I watched as Jensen tamped down the urge to roll his eyes.

Dad handed me an appetizer that looked something like a snail on a cracker and I discreetly slid it onto a cocktail napkin as a caterer passed. My new dress itched and I wished I'd taken the time to ask around the lab about these Spanx things I had on. From this first experience with them, I decided they were created by Satan, or a man who was too thin for skinny jeans.

"You're not just smart," Jensen was telling me. "You're fun. You're social. You're a pretty girl."

"Woman," I corrected in a mumble.

He leaned closer, keeping our conversation hidden from passing partygoers. Heaven forbid one of New York's high society should hear him giving me a lecture on how to be more socially slutty. "So I don't understand why we've been visiting you here for three days and the only people we've hung out with are *my* friends."

I smiled at my oldest brother, and let my gratitude for his over-protective-hyper vigilance wash over me before the slower, heated flush of irritation rose along my skin; it was like touching a hot iron, the sharp reflex followed by the prolonged, throbbing burn. "I'm almost done with school, Jens. There's plenty of time for life after this."

"*This* is life," he said, eyes wide and urgent. "*Right now.* When I was your age I was barely hanging on to my GPA, just hoping I would wake up on Monday and not be hung-over."

Dad stood silently beside him, ignoring that last remark but nodding at the general gist that I was a loser with no friends. I gave him a look that was meant to communicate, "*I get* this *coming from the workaholic scientist who spent more time in the lab than he did in his own house?*" But he remained impassive, wearing the same expression he had when a compound he expected to be soluble ended up a goopy suspension in a vial: confused, maybe a little offended on principle.

Dad had given me *drive*, but he always assumed Mom had given me even a little *charm*, too. Maybe because I was female, or maybe because he thought each generation should improve upon the actions of the one before, I was meant to do the whole career-life balance better than he had. The day Dad turned fifty, he'd pulled me into his office and said, simply, "The people are as important as the science. Learn from my mistakes." And then he'd straightened some papers on his desk and stared at his hands until I got bored enough to get up and go back into the lab.

Clearly, I hadn't succeeded.

"I know I'm overbearing," Jensen whispered.

"A bit," I agreed.

"And I know I meddle."

I gave him a knowing look, whispering, "You're my own personal *Athena Poliás*."

"Except I'm not Greek and I have a penis."

"I try to forget about that."

Jensen sighed and, finally, Dad seemed to get that this was meant to be a two-man job. They'd both come down to visit me, and although it had seemed a strange combination for a random visit in February, I hadn't given it much thought until now. Dad put his arm around me, squeezing. His arms were long and thin, but he'd always had the vise-like grip of a man much stronger than he looked. "Ziggs, you're a good kid."

I smiled at Dad's version of an elaborate pep talk. "Thanks."

Jensen added, "You know we love you."

"I love you, too. Mostly."

"But . . . consider this an intervention. You're addicted to work. You're addicted to whatever fast track you think you need your career to follow. Maybe I always take over and micromanage your life—"

"*Maybe*?" I cut in. "You dictated everything from when Mom and Dad took the training wheels off my bike to when my curfew could be extended past sunset. And you didn't even live at home anymore, Jens. I was *sixteen*."

He stilled me with a look. "I swear I'm not going to tell you what to do just . . ." he trailed off, looking around as if someone nearby might be holding up a sign prompting the end of his sentence. Asking Jensen to keep from micromanaging was like asking anyone else to stop breathing for ten short minutes. "Just call someone."

"'Someone?' Jensen, your point is that I have no friends. It's not *exactly* true, but who do you imagine I should call to initiate this whole get-out-and-live thing? Another grad student who's just as buried in research as I am? We're graduate students in biomedical engineering. It's not exactly a thriving mass of socialites."

He closed his eyes, staring up at the ceiling before something seemed to occur to him. His eyebrows rose when he looked back to me, hope filling his eyes with an irresistible brotherly tenderness. "What about Will?"

I snatched the untouched champagne flute from Dad's hand and downed it.

I didn't need Jensen to repeat himself. Will Sumner was Jensen's college best friend, Dad's former intern, and the object of every one of my teenage fantasies. Whereas I had always been the friendly, nerdy kid sister, Will was the bad boy genius with the crooked smile, pierced ears, and blue eyes that seemed to hypnotize every girl he met.

When I was twelve, Will was nineteen, and he came home with Jensen for a few days around Christmas. He was dirty, and—even then—delicious, jamming on his bass in the garage with Jensen and playfully flirting away the holidays with my older sister, Liv. When I was sixteen, he was a fresh college graduate and worked for my father over the summer. He exuded such raw, sexual charisma that I gave my virginity to a fumbling, forgettable boy in my class, trying to relieve the ache I felt just being near Will.

I was pretty sure my sister had *kissed* him—and Will was too old for me anyway—but behind closed doors, and in the secret space of my own heart, I could admit that Will Sumner was the first boy I'd ever wanted to kiss, and the first boy who eventually drove me to slip my hand under the sheets, thinking of him in the darkness of my own room.

Of his devilish playful smile and the hair that seemed intent on falling over his right eye.

Of his smooth, muscled forearms and tan skin.

Of his long fingers and even the little scar on his chin.

When the boys my age all sounded the same, Will's voice was deep, and quiet. His eyes were patient and knowing. His hands weren't ever restless and fidgety, they were usually resting deep in his pockets. He licked his lips when he looked at girls, and he made quiet, confident comments about breasts and legs and tongues.

I blinked, looking up at Jensen. I wasn't sixteen anymore. I was twenty-four, and Will was thirty-one. I'd seen him four years before at Jensen's ill-fated wedding, and his quiet, charismatic smile had only grown more intense, more maddening. I'd watched, fascinated, as Will slipped away into a coatroom with two of my sister-in-law's bridesmaids.

"Call him," Jensen urged, pulling me from my memories. "He has a good balance of work and life. He's local, he's a good guy. Just . . . get out some, okay? He'll take care of you."

I tried to quell the hum vibrating all along my skin when my oldest brother said this. I wasn't sure *how* I wanted Will to take care of me: did I want him to just be my brother's friend, helping me find more balance? Or did I want to get a grown-up look at the object of my filthiest fantasies?

"Hanna," Dad pressed. "Did you hear your brother?"

A waiter passed with a tray of full champagne flutes and I swapped out the empty one for a full, bubbly glass. "I heard him. I'll call Will."

See how Chloe and Bennett got together in the book that started it all...

More Than 2 Million Reads Online—FIRST TIME IN PRINT!
PICK UP OR DOWNLOAD YOUR COPY TODAY!
"The perfect blend of sex, sass, and heart!" –S. C. Stephens, bestselling author of *Thoughtless*
Beautiful
BASTARD
A Novel
CHRISTINA LAUREN

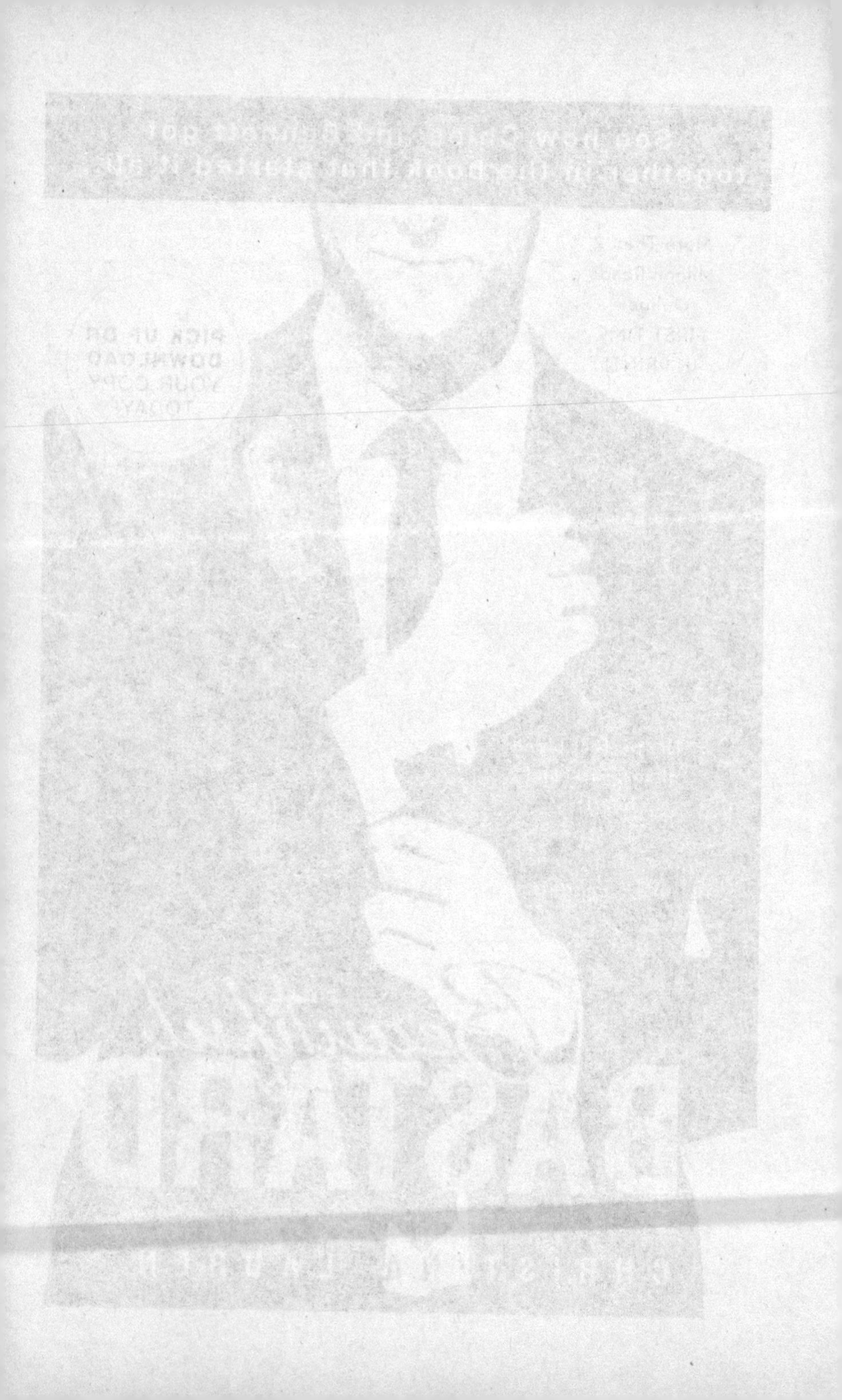

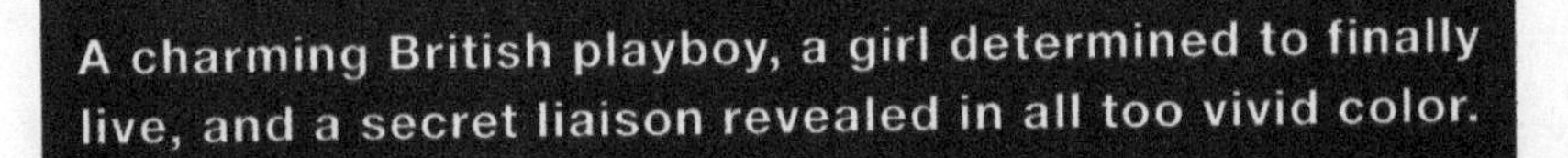

A charming British playboy, a girl determined to finally live, and a secret liaison revealed in all too vivid color.

"The perfect blend of sex, sass, and heart!"
—Bestselling author S. C. Stephens on *Beautiful Bastard*

PICK UP OR DOWNLOAD
YOUR COPY TODAY!

THE ALL-NEW, SCORCHING SEQUEL TO *BEAUTIFUL BASTARD*!

A Novel

Beautiful STRANGER

NEW YORK TIMES BESTSELLING AUTHOR
CHRISTINA LAUREN